Large

Ermin

Singing Tariat

W9-CRR-002

January 5, 2021

ωk

SINGING LARIAT

Center Point
Large Print

Also by Will Ermine and available
from Center Point Large Print:

Rustlers' Bend
Outlaw on Horseback
Plundered Range
The Drifting Kid

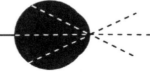

SINGING LARIAT

WILL ERMINE

CENTER POINT LARGE PRINT
THORNDIKE, MAINE

INTRODUCTION

The detective story and the Western are blood-cousins, so to speak, because of their common origin here in America. But they are also cousins in spirit. Both rely upon the love of adventure, the delight in the interplay of wit, the thrill to danger and to vigorous action that are rooted deep in the American character.

This is one of the reasons why I, who write detective novels, am also a reader of Westerns. For another, I am myself a Westerner. I live in the West, I work there, and, when I can, I travel there, seeking out the unexploited places where it is not hard to imagine a Western story still happening. This is a land I like, and when I read a novel by Max Brand or Zane Grey or Colt MacDonald, full of the odor of sage and the lure of wide horizons, I know the pleasures of recognition.

When asked to select this series of Triple-A Western Classics from the Morrow, Mill and Jefferson House lists, I decided at once that no such collection would be complete without Will Ermine. He is well known—and deservedly popular—both for his books and for his magazine stories, each one of which, swift-moving and realistic, maintains the true Western flavor. I have chosen SINGING LARIAT because to my mind it is one of Ermine's best. It is an exciting, virile story. Its characters are well drawn. The picture it gives of life in the Nebraska Territory right after the Civil War is fresh and colorful. And if you once start reading SINGING LARIAT, you will not put it down.

Erle Stanley Gardner

Temecula, California
June 1, 1948

CHAPTER ONE

With a noisy churning of paddle-wheels, her timbers trembling to the pound of her engines, the *Missouri Belle* crawled steadily up the broad, sluggish surface of the Missouri River. Her decks were colorful, under the beat of a strengthening spring sun, with brawny, two-fisted men who crowded everywhere, talking, laughing, arguing. Many showed themselves, by the faded uniforms they wore, to be ex-soldiers. Others were frontiersmen, freighters, trappers, scouts, bearded and keen of eye; men with the bark on.

On the texas deck stood a man, young in years, but with stern practicality in the set of his broad shoulders, whose glance scanned hungrily the low, characterless shore-line stretching far away on either side of the muddy brown waters. He was Salem Hardesty, mustered out of the Union ranks that spring. Six years had passed since he had laid eyes on the silent vastness of the West. Six long years filled with the memory of stinking trenches and poor food, of bursting shells and hand-to-hand fighting in the open, of endless marching and counter-marching, and always of more fighting. Seven years ago Hardesty had been a free trapper, a Mountain Man, roaming at will the broad Indian lands south of the upper Missouri. Now he was going back.

At his side stood a gnarled, homely little man, twenty years his senior, but with the same squinting eagle-look in his pale eyes. Texan was stamped all over him. Lone Benton—or Lone Star Benton, or Dave Benton—and he had been called all three names in the past—had been a cattleman before his convictions had thrown him into the Union forces under McClellan. Chance had flung him in Hardesty's way early in the war; and the hardships of that conflict, stoically shared, had ended by making them fast friends.

This morning Benton scrutinized the shores of the Missouri as narrowly as his companion. It was his first sight of the West. From his occasional grunts, and the square set of his jaw, it was plain he didn't think much of it. "Ain't seen any land to brag about yet," he muttered at last, in a suspicious tone.

"Wait," Hardesty counseled. "I promised you a country you'd think was heaven itself, Lone; you'll see it yet."

Benton's dour response was another grunt expressive of doubt. Hardesty would have said more, but at the moment a flurry occurred below on the main deck. They looked down there.

In the bow of the boat two men had started an argument. Both were six-footers. One wore a frayed coat of Confederate gray, the other, gray pants and a battered Confederate campaign hat. From their vehemence it was evident that they took their difference seriously. Without any warning, one of them swung violently on the other as men crowded forward. Hardesty caught the glint of a brandished knife. A yell rang out, curses.

The next moment a tall, husky man of self-confident mien broke through the ring. A sweep of his beam-like arm sent the antagonists staggering apart; the knife which a moment ago had threatened to draw blood, clattered on the deck.

"That'll be all of this," he rasped, authority in his tone. His cool glance swept the men crowding about. "Okay, boys—show's over."

Catching balance, the men he had separated glared fiercely, at a loss. For a moment it looked as if they meant to override him. The big fellow seemed to expect something of the sort.

"Ash," he told one of them levelly, "you and Pawnee forget it—or by God, I'll toss you both in the river!"

For a space the tension held. Then the man called Ash shrugged, turning away. Pawnee Failes muttered something which Hardesty didn't catch; and then Lone Benton's words broke in on his thoughts.

"Who is that big hombre, anyhow?" Lone growled.

"Rafe Perrine," Hardesty supplied. "Those

gents who started the fight belong to his crowd—"

"Yuh know Perrine, then?"

The answer was a curt nod. "He's a trapper. Virginian. Fought with Beauregard's column, till they made him a scout."

"What's he doin' out here?"

"I hear he's going back to trapping. He's formed his own company of half a dozen men." Hardesty's tone said what he thought would be the outcome of the venture.

The crowd on the foredeck below had broken up, Perrine returning to a card game in the crowded cabin. Hardesty and Lone Benton, with many others, returned to their study of the river banks. It was the Texan who pointed out the first signs of a distant town on the west bank, as they rounded a bend. "There she is," he exclaimed with deep interest, gaze sharpening.

Hardesty assented. "We'll soon be there."

Half an hour later the *Missouri Belle* churned up to the landing-stage at Nebraska City. She was accorded a noisy reception. Lines were flung out and made fast; the gangplank was lowered. Negro roustabouts attacked the piles of freight, shouting and singing; and passengers streamed off the boat to join the motley crowd on the bank and in the streets of the busy frontier town.

Hardesty and Benton saw to their own

belongings, including a full wagon-load of supplies and some saddles, at the Texan cut of which bearded traders and buckskin-clad hunters stared in puzzlement. Then the two headed up Nebraska City's main business street, Lone's shrewd eyes busily absorbing the unfamiliar scene. The place was filled with bustle and activity. Emigrants were everywhere, even to sunbonneted women and children. Benton's lip curled at the sight of stolid, blanketed Indians, begging tobacco, food, anything they could get.

Hardesty and himself were heading for a grog-shop, when suddenly the former paused. Toward them came a tall, lanky, iron-jawed man whom Hardesty recognized. At his side moved a slim, brown-haired girl who walked with lithe freedom; and it was on the latter that Salem's gaze was fixed. There was interest, almost hunger, in his eyes; before a word was spoken, the gnarled Texan had caught that much.

"Well, Hardesty, so ye came back," the lanky man greeted, a thick Scotch burr in his voice.

"I have," Hardesty agreed. He spoke warmly to the girl. And then, turning to Benton: "Lone, I want you to meet Colin MacKinney. He's a trader from the Sioux country, an old friend. And Glenna is—"

"Her father's daughter," the girl smiled, taking Lone's measure quietly, and seeming to approve of what she found. MacKinney was gazing at Benton also.

"Ye'll not be from this country," he hazarded. Lone shook his head.

"Texas," he said. "Catclaw, buck-brush, cow critters. It's a lot different!"

MacKinney's glance returned to Hardesty. "You're not plannin' to go back trappin' again? Because your old stampin' grounds have changed, my boy," he went on before the other could open his mouth.

"Changed?"

The trader's nod was dour. "Trapped out clean. It's six years, remember, since you packed out your last bale o' prime furs! I'm not sayin' ye'll no find an occasional beaver house; but there's no livin' to be had out o' the traps any more." He spoke reluctantly, but with a stern regard for the truth. "I've still got my post on the Chadron; I've come out for supplies only, and to give the lassie a change. But—" He shook his head, breaking off.

Hardesty said slowly: "I half suspected as much. The change was coming, even before the war. Jim Bridger saw it; and Carson and Herring and others . . . When are you going back?" he interrupted himself.

MacKinney said they were taking the *Missouri Belle* north to Plattsmouth that afternoon; there was a trail west from that point which made it easy for his wagons. "I've still plenty to do—but Glenna wants some things from the shops and I'll stay with her," he continued.

Hardesty saw his opening and grasped it. "Maybe I can help. You go ahead and do your work, and I'll stay with Glenna, help her with her packages."

If MacKinney was mildly surprised by the proposal, he was not displeased. "That'll be fine," he assented. "We'll meet at the hotel at dinner-time."

After talking a few minutes longer, he took his leave. At the same time, Lone broke away. "I'll be waitin' for yuh in here," he told Hardesty, nodding toward a saloon. It was so arranged. Hardesty and the girl moved down the street together.

Glenna was interested in everything she saw. It was not often she had a chance to return to civilization, even for a short visit; yet she found time to take approving stock of the tall, bronzed man at her side, with his dead black hair and cheerful blue eyes. They had been friends since she was a young girl; she was a woman now, and it interested her to note the change in her feelings toward him. Much about him, which had never before concerned her, was now of vital moment.

As for Hardesty, he had scarcely recognized Glenna at first glance, so great had been the change in her. Her brown, almost honey-colored hair held his gaze; her hazel eyes were warm, alight with intelligence; but it was her erectness and the proud way she carried her head that got home to him. He found himself asking many questions concerning the six years of his absence.

"Father's business has gone down and down," she said soberly, "until now it is nearly non-existent. It is the quietness I mind the most. Even the Indians stay away more than usual. Mostly they go to the White Clay reservation—"

"A reservation?" he caught her up. "That's new—"

She nodded. "It's on the White River, in Dakota Territory. Occasionally we see a company of soldiers from Fort Robinson; but that is all. It was hard, all during the war, to get news of what was going on; sometimes we waited weeks for information already months old."

He turned the talk smoothly to herself, and Glenna countered by asking about the campaigns in which he had taken part. The time passed swiftly; it was nearing noon by the time they reached the big wooden Missouri House, where MacKinney waited. He joined them on the veranda, taking Glenna's packages from Hardesty.

"I understood ye to say ye're going back to the Niobrara country?" he opened up, fixing Hardesty with a look which said he had been thinking the subject over. At the other's nod,

14

he questioned bluntly: "What'll you do there?"

"I aim to start a ranch," Hardesty smiled. He decided to reveal his plans, adding: "A cattle ranch. I know there's been none north of Colorado for years; and none above the Platte even now; but I was afraid the hills would be trapped out. Lone Benton is a cowman. I made arrangements for a beef herd at Leavenworth, on the way up the river. We'll drive the stuff out to the White and start raising cattle."

MacKinney's bushy brows rose in astonishment. "Mon, ye no can do that!" he exclaimed. "Why, that's Sioux country, an' the heart of it to boot . . . Ye show yerself more foolish than I thought!"

"Perhaps Salem has thought it all out, Father," Glenna interposed quickly. MacKinney scowled.

"Will thinkin' do any good?" he demanded. "I doubt it—" He shook his grizzled head. "Why are ye no more conservative, like Rafe Perrine? It's trappin' *he's* going back to. I ha'e doubts about his luck; but maybe he's no so foolish at that. He knows furs."

Glenna's stillness held the effect of a start, and her smile faded. She said: "Rafe Perrine, Father?"

He assented. "I saw him just now; he'll join us later for the trip to Plattsmouth on the *Belle*."

Hardesty said: "I've gone over the whole plan in my mind, Mac; talked it out with Benton. He believes we can make a go of it with cattle. So do

15

I. There's good water and plenty of it—and that rich buffalo grass—"

MacKinney's scowl deepened. "Have ye counted on Injun raids? They'll get into ye, sure. And what about the blizzards?"

Hardesty shrugged. "The buffalo stand it. There's usually good graze left bare on one side of the coulees."

"But what'll ye do with this beef?" the trader pursued keenly. "Eat it all yerself? . . . Annie Breen supplies all the cow meat us few folks in the country make away with," he reminded.

"Annie Breen!" Hardesty echoed, remembering. "Dublin Annie, you mean?" He was naming the wife of a settler who had lived in the Niobrara country, thirty miles from MacKinney's post, since the days of good trapping. "But what of Pat?"

MacKinney said: "Pat Breen went huntin' one day four years ago, an' never come home. He won't."

"And Annie stays on?"

The trader nodded. "She makes gloves fer soldiers, patches their clothes an' the like. An' butchers. Half a dozen steers, she an' Mike started with; now she's got a score or two there on Ghost Creek."

Hardesty waved a hand. "That answers your own question," he pointed out. "Stock *can* be raised in that country."

MacKinney said testily: "Ye know very well the Sioux won't go near Ghost Creek, for reasons of their own . . . But sayin' they'll leave you alone," he repeated, "what'll ye do with the stuff?"

Hardesty was surprised. "Why, the Union Pacific has started building. It'll be out there within a hundred miles of us in a year or two. I can ship my beef to market—"

"Pah!" the trader ejaculated. "Talk, all talk! Mon, the reelroad'll never cross that country, I promise ye! . . . Give up this mad plan to run beef critters to the end o' the world, Salem! O' course," he added candidly, "it's nothing to me. But I like ye."

Hardesty smiled. He shook his head. "Afraid I can't do that. It's too late to turn back. You tell me yourself the trapping is gone. That only confirms me in my intention—"

MacKinney gave up, pity and sadness in his look. "A'weel!" he sighed. "Ye'll no listen to a word, ye stubborn mon! I could almost wish ye success. But—" His final headshake said that the ranching project was doomed to inevitable failure. Glenna attempted to soften it with a smile; but Hardesty's enthusiasm had suffered a check.

MacKinney he knew to be nobody's fool. But, one of the last remnants of the Green River Fur Company, since he had drifted down out of Canada as a young man, the trader had never been anything else but a pioneer. Hardesty could only hope that the narrowness of his experience, where cattle were concerned, had warped his judgment.

He took leave of father and daughter a moment later, to go in search of Lone Benton, promising to see the MacKinneys again before they left that afternoon on the *Missouri Belle*. Strong in his mind, as he turned toward the grog-shop indicated by Lone, was the picture of solicitude in Glenna's eyes where his personal fortunes were concerned. Plainly she hoped for the best for him, yet feared the worst.

But all that was banished from Hardesty's mind suddenly and completely as he paused in the door of the grog-shop. What he saw within focused his attention sharply.

Lone Benton was in the place, as he expected. Half a dozen harsh-faced, jeering men had him backed against the bar. They were twitting him about the Union uniform he wore, trying to yank it off him. One of the sleeves was half-torn out of his coat and he showed other marks of a scuffle.

"Better go back to butternut, Texas," one of them laughed hoarsely. "That blue's the wrong color for yuh—it don't go with yore sunburn!"

"Hell, if he's goin' to be obstinate we'll jest undress him ourselves," another thrust in. "Grab his left leg, Cade—"

Hardesty saw Rafe Perrine then. He was

18

standing in the center of the group, a sardonic smile on his big features as he gazed at the Texan. He was doing nothing to halt the bull-baiting; rather his manner seemed to encourage it.

"Damn yuh, lay off!" Benton jerked out fiercely, as one of his tormenters made a grab at him. They were Perrine's trappers, Hardesty made no doubt; and he looked them over closely. Most of them had come out of the Confederate Army; pants or coats or battered campaign hats indicated as much. All were tough specimens; and yet, there was that about Perrine himself which said he was the most dangerous. Dark-complected and beefy, with snapping black eyes, there was a malicious twist to his lips.

"Better sing low, Benton," he advised, as Lone told them what he would do given the opportunity. "Maybe the boys'll be easier on yuh—"

"Hell, we ain't figgerin' to hurt him," one rasped. "All we want is them pants!" He made a grab, anchoring Lone's arm. Another grasped Lone around the waist. The pack closed in.

Benton struggled fiercely, but he had no chance. He went down with a muffled yell.

Hardesty sprang forward. With powerful jerks he flung Perrine's men right and left. One crashed into a table, smashing it; another measured his length on the floor with a jar that shook the walls. The rest relinquished their interest in Lone suddenly, scrambling away.

Helping Lone to his feet, Hardesty turned then to face Perrine. The latter stood, legs apart and hands folded on his chest, watching; that cynical smile, touched with insolence, still playing about his lips.

"Rememberin' old times, Perrine?" Hardesty snapped.

Rafe grunted: "What you mean?"

He knew what Hardesty meant, however. Seven years ago, in the Yellowstone country, he had started for Rendezvous carrying a bale of prime beaver belonging to Hardesty. The latter had never seen them again, nor the equivalent of their value which he had confidently expected. Perrine swore they had been stolen by marauding Snakes. There was nothing to be done, though Hardesty strongly suspected the Southerner of selling his furs and pocketing the money; but it had made bad blood between them and neither showed any inclination to forget, even after so long a time.

Hardesty made no effort to refresh Rafe's memory. Perrine's crowd was bunching around him; their looks were black now. Plainly they wanted to tear down both Lone and Hardesty. Hardesty said gratingly: "Get out of the way. We're goin' out of here on our feet—but the first gent who offers to lay a hand on either of us again, won't!"

There was a growl of rising wrath. It died abruptly as a Frontier Colt appeared in Hardesty's hand, the muzzle unwavering. Even Perrine seemed taken aback.

"Don't get on yore ear, Hardesty," he laughed, his voice oily. "Why, shucks! The boys was jest havin' a little fun. Benton spoiled it by losin' his temper—"

"By Godfrey, you'd lose more'n that if I had my way!" Lone blazed at him. Hardesty elbowed him to silence.

"I don't think much of your idea of fun," he told Perrine bluntly. "If it happens again I'll square accounts with you personal. Now get out of the way!"

Rafe shifted from one foot to the other. He began to talk persuasively; but Hardesty was walking straight toward him. The gun was pointed directly at Perrine's waistcoat. Suddenly he gave over, moving aside out of the line of fire. His men followed suit, scowling.

"If that's your attitude, Hardesty," Perrine whipped over, "I ain't likely to forget it! You'll be seein' me again!"

Hardesty nodded, steering Lone toward the door, muttering his wrath. "I'll be ready for you," was what Salem told Perrine thinly. No one could have missed the warning in his tone. It did not escape Perrine. He turned away with a sneer, but there was hate in his eyes, murder in his heart.

CHAPTER TWO

Eating dinner at a restaurant, Hardesty and Lone were in time to get down to the river bank before the *Missouri Belle* pulled away. MacKinney and his daughter were standing on the deck. Rafe Perrine was with them. Crossing the gangplank, Hardesty and his companion joined the group.

A frown flitted over Benton's hard-bitten features at sight of Perrine, but he said nothing. Hardesty scarcely noted the Southerner, his face inscrutable; yet he liked little the idea of Perrine journeying up the river with Glenna and the trader. Perrine's men were not in evidence just now, but they were aboard. Probably the girl would be thrown in their company most of the way west to the Indian country.

"Well, Hardesty, ye've no changed your mind, I take it?" MacKinney opened up.

Hardesty shook his head, smiling at Glenna. "Afraid I can't do that." The trader's commiseration was patent.

"Good luck to ye then," he sighed. "Ye'll need plenty, with dumb cow beasties in your care."

Perrine chuckled. MacKinney had explained Hardesty's intentions to him. "At least Hardesty won't have to worry about the Sioux," he remarked. "They'll welcome him with open arms!"

Salem shot him a glance. He knew what Perrine meant. If there was a retort hovering on his lips, Glenna forestalled it by saying quickly. "At least we'll hear of you when you arrive, Salem? You'll not be too far away from us?"

He shook his head. "A matter of half a day's ride." He had no intention of giving Perrine any better idea of where he expected to settle and start his ranch.

After a brief greeting to father and daughter, Lone had half turned away to watch the handling of freight coming aboard the steamer. At last he broke into the talk to say: "We better git ashore, Salem. They're aimin' to pull in the gangplank—"

It was so. The freight was aboard; wood for the boiler fires had been stowed. In a few minutes the *Missouri Belle* would swing away from the bank. Hasty good-byes were said, and last minute messages that suddenly seemed important. Hardesty and Lone ran down the gangplank just as the roustabouts laid hold of it.

The steamer whistle shrilled hoarsely. The boat forged out into the sluggish current. Good-byes were waved. But for long minutes after the steamer had passed beyond earshot, Hardesty stood on the bank with his gaze fixed on the

23

diminishing figure of Glenna MacKinney. At last the boat disappeared around a bend.

"Rafe Perrine," Lone muttered at last, as if summing the man up. "If we don't never lay eyes on him again, that'll be soon enough!"

Whatever Hardesty's thoughts were on the subject, he kept them to himself, turning away.

A day passed, and another, without any sign of the herd of steers Hardesty expected from down river. But he knew it would be slow in coming, nor was he mistaken. It was a week later, and he and Benton were heartily tired of such amusements as Nebraska City afforded, when one afternoon a dust cloud appeared to the south and rolled slowly forward. It was Hardesty's beef.

He and Lone had procured tough, wiry Indian broncs which the Texan said would do. Hastily saddling up, they rode out to examine the stock. There were upward of eight hundred head in the bunch, mostly three and four year olds in fair condition. In purchasing them, Hardesty had avoided the runty, stringy, long-horn breed in favor of a graded, bigger-boned stock developed in the north of Texas.

They were in charge of a lean Texan with a drawl thick as cold sorghum; with him were four squinting, sun-and-wind-burned punchers who must have been born within hail of the Alamo. Their leader eyed Hardesty with steady curiosity, and said: "Heah's yo beef-critters, Hardesty.

24

Would yo' mind tellin' a man what y'all aimin' to do with so many up heah?"

"I'm startin' a cow ranch," was the answer. "West in the Indian lands."

"Lo'd, Lo'd!" the other exclaimed, staring his amazement. "Man, you ah plumb askin' fo' grief!"

Hardesty affected surprise, glancing at the other Texans who had come up. "Think so?" he countered. "I was figurin' to ask you boys if you'd consider goin' with me—"

He must have used just the right tone, for one of the others spoke up at once. "Reckon I wouldn't mind . . . Pony Johnson," he introduced himself. "I'm plumb t'ard of catclaw an' sand—an' fordin' the Red right reg'lar," he added.

Another seconded: "Count me in, if yo're a mind to. I'm Rusty Gallup."

Pleased, Hardesty glanced inquiringly at the others. A third man, Red Tyler, signified his willingness to go along—"If you'll wait till I get my bedroll out of the wagon!" The remaining two, however, were reluctant. One had obligations in Kansas; the other, if there was anything in the sly jibes of his friends, was remembering a girl who waited for him in Wilbarger County.

"Well," said Hardesty musingly, "with Johnson, Gallup and Tyler, that'll make five of us." Lone Benton nodded approval.

"We'll make do," was his comment.

Accordingly, Hardesty decided to lose no time about striking west. He spent the remainder of the day making ready the wagon-load of supplies they must take with them, and hired a lanky, horse-necked boy of seventeen, at a loose end, who could drive the team and said he knew how to cook.

Before dawn the following morning, the herd strung out across the rolling prairie on the first leg of the long drive across Nebraska Territory. It gave little trouble the first day, or on the next. At this season the sun still carried only a mild warmth; prairie grass was plentiful; and there was no shortage of creek water. But on the third day the steers moved slower. They were trail-weary. Lone told Hardesty it was no more than to be expected; and yet the latter grew warily alert.

It would not be long now before they began to cross the trail of small bands of Indians busily engaged in the spring hunt. More than once Hardesty asked himself with some uneasiness what the result of the first meeting would be. He knew the attitude the Sioux would take—that he was helping himself to their land. But the Ogalalas had always been friendly with him. He could only hope that that attitude would not change.

In the interests of avoiding unnecessary com-plications, however, either Hardesty himself, or one of the others, took to ranging a mile or more ahead of the steers, scanning the endless folds and coulees for the first sign of Indians. Hardesty would not be above turning the herd if it would serve to delay the inevitable.

Late that afternoon Salem mounted a low ridge in advance of the stock, and sat staring ahead so long that at length Lone rode up to join him. In view of the other's unfamiliarity with cattle, Benton had assumed the direction of the drive.

"Spot somethin'?" he queried.

Hardesty nodded without looking around. "Buffalo, I think," he responded. "A big herd. The sun's so low I can't see very well—"

Lone squinted west, shading his eyes with a hand. What he saw fetched a grunt of surprise from him. For more than a mile across the far horizon stretched a moving dark line.

"Buffler, shore's shootin'!" Lone exclaimed. "An' what's more, they're comin' this way!"

At Hardesty's suggestion, they struck in the spurs and rode forward, making for higher ground from which they could see more clearly. No sooner had they reached the spot than Hardesty whirled his bronc sharply.

"Those buffaloes are stampedin', Lone!" he cried. "There's Indians behind 'em! In ten minutes they'll be on our steers, if we don't do somethin'!"

There was no need to add what would be the result if the beef herd became mixed with the

27

shaggy, oncoming horde. Not only would they be lost to recovery, but many would be trampled to death.

The men lost no time in racing back to join the trail herd. Hardesty's quick glance took stock of their situation as he rode. They were in a country of low ridges, broken here and there by shallow canyons. One of the latter, slashing high ground a half mile to the north, caught his attention. He pointed to it.

"Swing 'em!" he yelled to Pony Johnson, who was riding point. "Make for that break and shove the stuff like hell!"

Galvanizing into action without question, with their help Johnson did as he was directed. But the steers refused to run, breaking into a trot which slackened after a few minutes. Lone jerked out: "You, Gallup! Tyler! Prod them cows! There's a buffler herd that'll be on our tails in no time! Hump yoreselves, or by God, I'll do it fer yuh!"

His words were needless, however. Beneath the restless bellowing of the steers, almost drowning the sound out even at this distance, there grew an ominous rumbling. It was the pound of thousands of hoofs.

A moment later, over the crest of a low rise to the west appeared an unbroken wall of buffalo. Huge, ungainly, they raced toward the cowboys at express-train speed. The cowboys yelled and began firing their guns; to Hardesty it appeared

28

impossible that the sanctuary of the canyon could be reached in time. There flashed across his mind the fact that he had sunk almost his last dollar in these steers. Were they to be swept away so soon?

The ground trembled as though under bombardment. A dust pall arose to obscure the unbroken wave of buffalo which poured forward. Terror, communicating itself to the steers like fire running in dry grass, swept them into a mad run. The men had only to guide them toward the canyon's mouth.

Once there they would be safe, since the buffalo split around the rocky ridge like water around an island. The first steers arrived; the punchers whipped up the drag. The buffalo were so near now, running head down, that Hardesty could hear their snorting. He whirled. A big bull, in advance of the others, crashed into the steers, sending one screaming to its knees. Hardesty shot; but the sixgun slug was no more than a fly sting to the buffalo. It forged on. Another steer went down. Then the last swept into the canyon, the men with it; and the dark tide of buffalo closed in.

Hardesty had not forgotten the Indians. He had caught the merest glimpse of feathered riders, and they had not seen him at all; but he had no time for them now. The steers were not yet entirely beyond danger. Only the roughness of the canyon, winding back upon itself, prevented them from rushing on to destruction. The air was thick with dust; he could see little or nothing. But he had to do what he could.

In the end, the rumble of buffalo hoofs ahead, as well as behind, turned the stock back. It milled in helpless terror, jamming the canyon. Hope came back to Hardesty. There was a chance yet that he could save his beef.

It was half an hour before the ground-shaking rumble began to slacken. The sun had sunk; dusk was thickening. Lone Benton joined Hardesty in the lower canyon, his face streaked and stained with dirt. But he was grinning.

"Them Injuns," he said. "Can't find a sign of 'em. I reckon they're plumb gone!"

Hardesty sighed his relief. "It's just as well. We'll haze the steers out of here, shove on to water and bed down for the night."

It was so done. Two miles took them to a shallow creek, muddied by the passage of the stampeding buffalo, but already clearing. There was enough grass to satisfy the steers. But they were growing gaunt from the long drive. Benton looked them over, his face thoughtful.

"Much farther to go?" he asked Hardesty.

"Two or three days should see us there," the latter answered. "We can take it easy—"

Lone nodded. "We'll have to."

It was as much for that reason as any other that,

by mid-morning on the following day, they ran into a traveling band of Ogalala Sioux. There were too many of them to fight successfully, and Hardesty rode out to parley with the chief, while the Texans bunched the steers and held them.

Fortunately, this was Long Hunter's band. Hardesty knew the chief; had trapped more than one winter season in his country, and was on easy terms with him. He raised a hand in greeting, coming up with every appearance of confidence and amity.

"How," said Hardesty, giving the proper amount of grunt to the greeting. "Long Hunter is well. His children are many, his ponies fat."

The chief eyed him keenly. There was undeniable dignity in his bronze impassiveness.

"Beaver Skin is well," he responded, giving Hardesty his Indian name. "But he has strange friends." His hawklike glance strayed toward the herd.

Salem smiled. "Long Hunter knows beef, which eats sweet and strays not far from camp. Beaver Skin has brought his herd with him."

The Ogalala thought inscrutably. "They graze on Indian land," he said suddenly. Hardesty pretended surprise.

"True," he admitted. "But Long Hunter has much land. Beaver Skin wants but little—" A stubborn look appeared on the coppery visage.

"Why does he ask for any?" he demanded.

Hardesty let the question hang in the air a while. "Long Hunter is right," he said at last. "Beaver Skin will pay toll. How much does Long Hunter ask?"

This required earnest consideration. Instead of answering at once, the chief retired to discuss the matter with his men. They took their time over it, finally deciding that ten head of steers would be enough. Hardesty bit his lips on hearing the verdict. But there was nothing for it but to comply. He rode back to join the punchers.

"What do they say?" Lone demanded tensely.

Hardesty said: "Cut out ten of the weakest steers—"

They stared at him. "Yuh mean yo're givin' them devils ten head?" Pony Johnson jerked out. "Why, dang their hides, what they *oughta* have is a dose of hot lead!"

Hardesty said: "Never mind. Do as I say."

They would have argued the matter, but he wouldn't hear of it. Grumbling, the punchers followed instructions, not without hostile glares in the direction of the Indians. The band paid no heed. They drifted on presently, driving the ten steers.

Little was said during the remainder of the day, but that night in camp the subject was reopened.

"Yo're makin' a mistake, Hardesty!" Pony Johnson declared. "Start somethin' like this, an' you'll soon be givin' yore shirt away. Dang the sneakin' renegades, I say; I know 'em!"

"Pony's right, Hardesty," Rusty Gallup seconded. "This is nothin' new to us. The Comanches tried that game down south, till we put a stop to it. Don't even start it up here; we're warnin' yuh!"

Hardesty showed his willingness to reason, pointing out that the friendship of these Indians might prove invaluable; but he got nowhere. Even Lone Benton doubted his wisdom.

"Bring the Injuns up short an' sharp," he counseled. "Yo're in this business to make money, Sale. Why, yuh kin give away more beef in a month, this way, than yore whole year's natural increase will amount to!"

Yet Hardesty clung to his own opinion of his proper course. He knew that white men owed the Indians more than a few head of stock. If he was scrupulous in his dealings with them, he hoped they might allow him to remain in the country unmolested. Once the Indian raids started, there would be no end of trouble. It might even be impossible to ranch under such conditions.

But if he had made up his mind, the Texans were no less wrathy when, the following day, another ten steers were handed over to a second band of Indians. Pony Johnson even went so far as to throw his hat on the ground violently.

"That settles it!" he swore. "I thought yuh was

takin' a big chance, Hardesty, comin' way out here. Now I know yo're a danged fool!"

Hardesty whirled on him in a flash. "Get your roll out of the wagon, Johnson," he directed curtly. "You're done. You can head back for the river right now!"

Pony's jaw dropped. "Yuh mean—I'm fired?"

"Yes; and I ought to set you afoot!"

But it was not his own predicament that interested Johnson. He still stared at Hardesty in amazement. "Yuh got guts," he managed admiringly; "stuck way out here, hundreds uh miles from anywheres, with eight hundred steers—an' still willin' to give a man his time fer shootin' off his mouth! . . . I'm takin' back what I said, Hardesty. An' I'll stick with yuh, if that's okay—at least till yuh ain't got no more cows to give to the Injuns," he concluded with an engaging grin.

Hardesty did not soften in the slightest.

"All right," he said. "But if you go on with me, I want it distinctly understood that like it or not, I'm boss here. My word goes!"

"Gotcha," Pony assented cheerfully. "I ain't tellin' yuh yore business no more."

Hardesty ran his eye over the others. No one had anything to say. He let the matter drop.

But that the subject of paying toll to the Indians was a sore one with him was plain when, later in the afternoon, Lone Benton dropped back from a ridge to the fore, with word that still another band of Sioux were waiting a few miles ahead.

"It's a game, Sale!" Lone warned thinly. "These redskins are passin' the word along to their friends that our beef is free fer the askin'. They'll plumb clean yuh out if yuh let it go on!"

Hardesty brushed the words aside with an impatient gesture. Nor did he ride ahead as he had done before, to parley with the waiting Indians.

They came in sight a few minutes later. From the way they surveyed the herd, their confident expectations were patent. Tightening up in spite of themselves, the punchers looked to Hardesty for instructions. Would he hand over more of his steers, they were wondering, or would he kick over the traces at last?

Rusty Gallup came jogging along the flank of the herd, his unsheathed rifle resting across his saddlebow. His face was flinty, his eyes a cold and hostile blue.

"What are yuh goin' to do now, Hardesty?" he muttered.

"That," was the gritted answer, "is precisely what those Indians are goin' to be askin' themselves in about two minutes!"

The punchers, strung taut with readiness, exchanged swift glances across the bobbing backs of the steers. A moment later the carved bronze chief, feathers jutting in his hair and a blanket thrown loosely over his shoulder, pushed out from the band astride a hawk-like pinto pony to meet Hardesty.

CHAPTER THREE

"Beaver Skin," the Indian opened up woodenly, "you are on my land. I own it." He swept his arm around, full circle. "As far as the sun shines, the land is mine."

The direction of his talk was plain; it was made plainer by his significant glance in the direction of the steers. Hardesty said: "That is right, Rides Far. Beaver Skin is envious as he rides by. Is the hunting good?"

The chief was not to be put off so easily. "Beef," he told Hardesty levelly, looking him in the eye, "is good to eat. For ten of these poor-looking animals, Rides Far will trade ten fat buffalo, which Beaver Skin may catch whenever he pleases."

Hardesty reddened at the bare-faced proposition. But he only shook his head. "Beaver Skin is sorry," he responded regretfully; "but his answer is no."

Stolidly persistent, the Indian only sat and stared blandly. A despot in his own little world, he was accustomed to getting what he wanted. "Rides Far," he grunted coolly, "wants ten beef. Beaver Skin will give them to him—"

Hardesty exploded sharply: "I will like hell!"

37

He gestured sharply. "I've got nothing to give you. Go on your way!"

If the chief was surprised, he failed to show it. After a full minute, to show that it was by choice, he turned his pony and jogged slowly away. With Lone at his side, Hardesty anxiously awaited the result of his firmness. Rides Far joined his band, and for some minutes there was a guttural discussion. Then the Indians started to ride off.

"Wal," Lone growled. "That's that—"

He got no further. Suddenly a rifle cracked. One of the braves had fired; the slug whined overhead. There were more shots. In a twinkling the Indians were racing along the flank of the herd, lying low over the ponies' withers. Their hostile design was plain. Hardesty cursed.

"Let 'em have it!" he cried. "We ain't swallowin' this!"

Almost before he spoke, the punchers swung into action. Rusty Gallup's rifle exploded sharply. The others were not far behind him. The advantage was all with them from the start. Not only did they mean business, but they were accustomed to shooting straight.

An Indian let out a screech as his bronc went down. He sprang off just in time. Two bounds, and he was scrambling up behind another brave. The band was swinging round the flank of the herd now. They meant to circle the bunch, using the method by which many a wagon train had been cut off. Hardesty jerked out:

"Straight at them! Cut 'em off!"

He was the first to start, firing as he rode. The punchers streaked after him. The boldness of the attack was a surprise to the savages. With wild yells they broke and swung away. Their ponies were fleet. Even so, Hardesty saw one brave tumble out of the fight, limbs flying. Another went down.

"Smoke 'em!" Lone Benton yelled fiercely. "By God, we'll give 'em a bellyful of this!"

Other Indians swung back in an effort to pick up the fallen. The guns of the punchers concentrated on them. Only by the narrowest margin, and clinging to the sides of the ponies as they sprang astride and dug in their heels, were the savages able to escape the fate of their luckless companions. The dead were left lying in the tall grass.

The punchers would have pressed on in pursuit of the yelling fugitives, but Hardesty would not allow it.

"We'll stay with the steers," he ruled, calling them back. Johnson and the others knew he was right.

Turning back, they had their look at the dead Ogalalas. Hardesty got down and pulled a carbine out from under one of them. "I thought they were usin' somethin' better than trade muskets," he grunted, holding the weapon out.

The others stared at it. "Why, that's a Spencer!" Lone exclaimed, "—a .56 caliber. What the hell?"

"Somebody's passin' out arms to the dang redskins!" Rusty Gallup summed up the thought of them all. Benton nodded.

"And an army issue at that," he added tersely, pointing to the Confederate insignia, CSA, stamped in the stock of the gun. He raised his eyes, and they met Hardesty's unwavering gaze. Suddenly, the same suspicion was in the minds of both.

"Rafe Perrine," Lone muttered. "Was it *trappin'* he claimed him an' his bunch was out here for?"

Hardesty said colorlessly: "Yeh."

There was no more to be learned here. Thrusting the Spencer under the straps of his saddle, Hardesty remounted and turned back toward the herd. The others followed. Kezzy Sparrow, the boy who had been hired to drive the supply wagon, had come up, attracted by the firing. He was full of questions. The punchers joshed him about being so far to the rear when trouble struck. They only succeeded in magnifying the chagrin of the boy, who possessed all the bloodthirstiness of his age.

"Never mind, Kez," Hardesty told him grimly. "You'll see plenty of Sioux chasin' before you're much older!"

The steers were pushed on without delay.

Despite their condition, Lone would not hear of their taking it easy, saying the quicker they reached what was to be their home range, now, the better it would be.

Against all expectation, no more Indians were seen that day, nor on the next. Late in the afternoon the character of the land changed. Hills were higher and more numerous, carved by pleasant creeks; patches of pines, of willow and alder, began to appear. Hardesty kept a careful watch ahead.

As for the Texans, they were deeply gratified by the appearance of this country, with its endless buffalo grass, and rich in water. Not even the hazards of the clay banks bothered them.

"Reckon I didn't expect to see anythin' like this," Lone admitted to Hardesty. "It's good 'nough right around here to raise steers big as bufflers!"

His answer was a smile. But all Hardesty would say was the one word: "Wait."

Shortly afterward he drew rein on a grassy swell and waved an arm. "There's the Chadron," he told Lone. "MacKinney's post is only a mile or two farther." Despite the quietness of his voice, he found a thrill in the knowledge.

The sun was swinging low when they halted the herd on a grassy flat half a mile from MacKinney's Fort. While the punchers stood guard, Hardesty and Lone rode in to pick up a few things which the former thought they needed.

The trading post was a log affair standing beside the creek. It had a stockade which stood in some need of repairs. The broad gate was propped open. The two jogged into the yard.

The post itself was not large. Oblong in shape, with a slightly slanting sod roof, it had few windows, but was pierced high up by what had obviously been meant for loop-holes. Freight wagons stood about the yard, empty and waiting the next trip out for supplies. There was a dark-visaged Indian working about a lean-to at the back.

Even as Hardesty and Lone arrived, Glenna MacKinney stepped out of the door. Salem's gaze took her in hungrily. From the flounced and ribbon-trimmed dress she had worn in Nebraska City, she had reverted to fringed buckskin skirt and plain woollen blouse; but the change, if anything, made her more handsome. If it was not the effect of the honey-colored hair, her hazel eyes held a remarkable warmth.

"You have arrived at last!" she greeted Hardesty. "Now I can admit I was somewhat worried about you—"

The knowledge gave him unaccustomed pleasure; yet even so, he noted that she did not ask whether they had had any trouble. Glenna said:

"Father is not very far away. Get down and stretch your legs while I find him."

Swinging to the ground, Hardesty and Lone stepped to the door of the trade room. It was piled and hung with a variety of necessities; Benton had not seen anything like it since visiting the Santa Fe country in his boyhood. He gazed around. For Hardesty, the place held a host of memories. More than once he had outfitted here for lonely months in the mountains; and there were pictures as well of Glenna as a girl, which he was of no mind to shirk because the child had given place to the woman.

Both were thus occupied when MacKinney entered through a rear door. Glenna was with him. Even as they spoke, Hardesty found time to note that the trader wore no smile. His expression was sober, his glance sharp.

"So ye got as far as this, then," he said as if surprised by the fact.

"Did you really think we wouldn't?"

MacKinney nodded woodenly. "I'll admit as much, an' no bones about it. But," he shook his head now, gravity deepening, "your troubles are no over. Dinna think it!"

Hardesty raised his brows.

"This killin' ye thought fit to do for a handful o' cows," the trader threw at him suddenly. "I know all about it. What do ye mean by it, Hardesty?"

Salem saw Glenna's hand steal to her father's elbow as if to restrain him, for his voice had risen.

"Rides Far has come to you?" Hardesty's tone was level. "His braves fired on us, Mac. We shot back." He stood his ground with that.

MacKinney reddened. Plainly he had intended to curb his indignation; but the other's tone did nothing to help him.

"*Why* did they fire on ye?" he flared sharply. "That's the point!"

"Because I refused to give them my steers."

MacKinney strove to appear scornful. "An' for two or three cows, ye—"

"Ten cows," Hardesty inserted flatly. "I had already given twenty head. Perhaps that was my mistake."

Benton jerked his chin down in agreement, following the talk closely. "An' a bad one," he murmured. MacKinney, however, might never have heard him. He was staring at Hardesty bitterly.

"I gave ye better sense," he cried. "Are cows, then, worth the lives of men—even if they be savages?" Before Hardesty could reply, he rushed on: "But that's only part of it! Ye threw lead at friends—braves who've treated ye square enough in the past. Ye raised hell, Hardesty, that's what! An' on top of it all, ye come here!"

Hardesty was taken aback by his vehemence. When he had made his decision to pay no more toll—or extortion—to Rides Far, and had carried the decision through to its consequences, it had

44

never struck him that the occurrence might carry an echo in this direction. His glance leaped to Glenna's face.

The girl was giving all her attention to the trader. "Father, must you be so harsh? Salem has done no more than he felt he must. I am sure of it!"

MacKinney shook her off, his ire running away with him.

"We'll come to the bottom of this," he declared doggedly. "I've my own position to consider. There's no half a dozen of us here if the Sioux come raidin' and shootin'; we would'na stand a ghost of a show! I'll no have it, I tell ye! I've always been friends with the Indians; I mean to go on being. As for you—" he shot a lean finger at Hardesty, "—if this is the road ye choose, shootin' and standin' off all comers, and to hell with what happens, ye better go on your way now! I want no steers at my post now or later. Understand me!"

Hardesty must have been obtuse indeed to have failed in that. Still he strove to present his own point of view. MacKinney refused to listen.

"I've said my say, an' ye'll like it fine," was his last word. Clearly his stand in the matter was iron; he was anxious only to see the last of Hardesty and his steers.

The latter shrugged helplessly, giving Glenna an apologetic look. That she thought her father

45

hard was evident; his word had always been law at this isolated trading post, however. It could be no different now. Her glance seemed to plead with Hardesty to understand her position.

Salem nodded as if to himself. But there was more to it than this difference with an old acquaintance. He wondered how the unfortunate affair would affect Glenna's interest in him. Would she find a welcome for him the next time he came? For even now, it did not occur to him that the sensible course would be to stay away altogether. He must depend on MacKinney's Fort for various supplies whether he liked it or not.

Recalling that he stood in need of a few items even now, he named them. As if there was no more to say, MacKinney got the things out, receiving Hardesty's pay for them in dour silence.

"Well—" In spite of himself, Hardesty felt the strong impulse to linger. He wanted to talk with Glenna at least. Yet it was patent the time for that was not propitious. "I expect we'd better get along," he concluded awkwardly.

Lone appeared of more than half a mind to state his opinion of MacKinney in no uncertain terms. A glance at the girl's distressed face changed his intention. With a grunt he swung toward the door; and telling father and daughter good-bye, Hardesty followed. MacKinney came after as if to see them off the place.

A horseman entered at the gate as they reached the yard. He sat his saddle freely and easily, and there was insolent self-assurance in his bearing; something leaped in Hardesty as he recognized Rafe Perrine.

Perrine was alone. The look he bent on Hardesty and Lone was vaguely mocking, but he nodded pleasantly enough.

"Hear you had some trouble getting here, Hardesty," he remarked.

Salem's jaw unconsciously squared and a glint appeared in his eye. Whether Perrine had divined from the look on their faces the nature of the situation into which he had ridden, was uncertain; but if the man had deliberately chosen to step on sore toes with his first words, he could scarcely have succeeded better.

"Thanks to you," Hardesty retorted curtly, sure the other knew all about the brush with the Sioux. Perrine appeared genuinely surprised at his answer.

"Me?" he said quickly. "What have I got to do with it?" But Hardesty was done with that angle of the matter. Perrine had ridden close, still sitting his saddle; and Hardesty's glance was fixed on the stock of the rifle which protruded from his saddle-boot.

"Isn't that a Spencer?" he queried shortly.

Perrine glanced down. His self-control was admirable as he responded coolly: "Yeh, it is."

47

"Thought so," Salem continued tunelessly. "A .56 caliber, too."

Perrine's eyes hardened. "Jest what is all this leadin' to?" he demanded. Instead of answering, Hardesty met his gaze squarely and tapped the rifle-stock with his finger.

"You've got some more of these, haven't you?"

The Southerner stiffened. It was impossible wholly to avoid the thin significance in Hardesty's words. Lone Benton was eyeing him with undisguised hostility; and even MacKinney and the girl, mystified no little by the strange turn the talk had taken, were arrested, waiting for what was to come.

Perrine jerked out harshly: "Suppose yuh come to the point of all this, Hardesty!"

For answer, the latter wheeled to step swiftly to the side of his own bronc, tethered at the hitch-rail before the trading post. With a single motion he twitched out the Spencer carbine taken from the dead Ogalala. Turning then, he thrust the gun out to Perrine, stock first.

"Here's one of your toys," he dropped flatly. "One of your men—lost it!"

Perrine took the weapon, pretended to examine it in a puzzled way.

"What's it all mean?" he asked with studied bewilderment. "Where did yuh get this gun?"

"Figure it out for yourself," Hardesty told him. It was plain that this was his last word. Turning on his heel, he murmured: "Let's go, Lone." With Benton following suit, he swung astride his pony and headed for the gate, the hoofs of the horses sounding loud in the weighty silence.

CHAPTER FOUR

It was near dusk when Hardesty and Benton pulled away from MacKinney's Fort, but the former said they would push the steers on for a few miles. While he took no stock in the trader's fears for his safety, Hardesty intended to give the other no added cause for grievance.

The punchers stared when he gave the word to shove on, but at a warning look from Lone, they did as they were told. In the first dark the herd was bunched in a grassy coulee a few miles north of the Chadron. Kez Sparrow soon had a hot meal ready. Such cooking skill as he boasted of had been exaggerated; but hungry as they were from the long hours on the trail, the men seldom bothered to comment.

Sitting around the fire after supper, Hardesty cheered them with the announcement that tomorrow would see them at their destination.

"Right around here'd suit me as well as anywhere," Lone averred. He was full of admiration for this country, the like of which he had plainly feared they would never see. "Must be a catch in it some'eres," he concluded. "After west Texas, this is most too good to be true. I reckon the Injuns is the answer."

Hardesty felt no inclination to smile. He knew only too well that they had not heard the last of their clash with the Ogalala Sioux. There was also Rafe Perrine to consider. The incident of the Spencer carbines was too pointed to pass over. Hardesty had no doubt that Perrine's talk of trapping had been no more than a blind; that the Southerner's real object was the smuggling of rifles and whisky to the Indians.

Risky as this illicit trade must be, there was a large profit in it. Unscrupulous men could always be found to pick up an easy dollar, regardless of the consequences. Embittered by the outcome of the late war, in which he had fought on the losing side, Perrine would have no scruples about adding to the troubles of the Army in the West.

Nor had Hardesty forgotten Perrine's personal enmity. Whether or not Rafe would go out of his way for it, he would not let pass any chance to make trouble that came ready to hand. The fact rendered Hardesty even more restless than usual.

"We're standin' double guard tonight," he decided. "Kez can do his trick too. I don't propose to run the risk of a slip-up now."

No one made any demur. While the first night guard saddled up and started for the herd, the others rolled in their blankets. Nothing untoward occurred, however. The guard was changed at midnight, and Hardesty pulled on his boots to take his turn; he was on watch still when the first dawn light streaked the east.

Sunrise saw the steers on their way again. Hardesty was anxious to reach the ground he had settled on for his ranch. He knew it well; in his mind's eye he saw it as he had last seen it: a strip twenty miles long by half as wide, between the White River and the Niobrara. It was in the very heart of the main camping ground of the Ogalala Sioux. In itself this was something to think about; but the land was such that, if it came to that, it was well worth fighting to hold.

The day proved uneventful. The steers traveled slowly now, but Hardesty discounted somewhat his own impatience. The trail led over grassy plains country, in itself nothing to exclaim over; but the season of the year, which was at its mildest, the vast over-arching sky with its floating white clouds, which seemed to enclose a land literally endless in extent, breathed of peace.

Lone was not missing a thing. "Ain't far south of the Black Hills here, are we?" he queried.

Hardesty shook his head. He knew what the other was thinking. At intervals during the last year, even in the far bivouacs of the Northern Army, they had heard occasionally of the excitement occasioned by the discovery of gold in the Black Hills. It was land belonging to the Indians, and assigned to them specifically by treaty; but that did not deter the restless Argonauts. Even now they were flocking to the diggings over the northern trails; Deadwood had been built, to become a wide-open, roaring town overnight; the Indians, fought off repeatedly, persisted in claiming the hills. Their raids spread destruction everywhere.

"Hundred miles or so," said Hardesty. "Far enough so we'll be left alone, with any luck."

There was no stop for the noon meal. All were anxious to lay eyes on what was to be their new stamping ground. In the middle of the afternoon the herd mounted a high ridge and Hardesty waved an arm toward the country beyond.

"There's our ranch," he declared with deep satisfaction.

The others reined up to gaze. For some moments no word was said. There was small need for comment.

Below them lay the lush green valley of the Niobrara. It was a rolling hill country that spread beyond, prettily parked with pines. Even from here they could tell that grass was plentiful, the juicy nutritious buffalo grass so highly prized for the raising and fattening of beef.

Lone was the first to find his voice. "Man, there must be a spring in nigh every other gulch, there!" he exclaimed. "What a range!"

Pony Johnson said: "Cast yore eye over them white cliffs hemmin' the valley in! Why, winter or summer, there ain't nothin' to beat this place!"

He was right. The high limestone bluffs which guarded the country made an ideal protection against the raw blasts of winter storm. In summer they threw a grateful shade. At all times they constituted a natural range boundary which could be calculated to save an endless amount of riding.

Pleased at the enthusiasm with which his choice had been received, Hardesty led the way down the ridge through a gap and to the river, which presented no obstacles to easy fording. An hour before sundown the steers spread out and began to graze on the hills, still carpeted with spring flowers.

Camp was thrown up beside the river. The talk around the fire that evening was animated.

"I shore gotta take back anythin' I ever thought about the country yuh promised," Benton grinned to Hardesty. "Yuh never said it'd be anything like this. Good thing yuh didn't—I'd never've believed yuh!"

The others were fully as generous with their approval. As for Hardesty, he was anxious now to locate a site and begin to throw up his ranch buildings. There was even more intense satisfaction than he had expected in building his own spread. The fact that he was the first man ever to start a ranch north of the Platte, almost disappeared in the pleasure of the work.

Originally a New Englander, with the stamp of the trapper on him, Hardesty was still a novice where the handling of cattle was concerned. Scarcely a day passed that the Texans did not frankly laugh at him for some mistake. But he was catching on quickly. The day would come, Lone Benton declared, when Salem would be as good a cowman as any of them. It was high praise, coming from him.

The night guard was not relaxed because they were no longer on the trail. Hardesty had no idea how long it would be before his presence here was discovered by the Ogalalas; it would not be long. After that, events would have to take care of themselves and there was not a man in the outfit who didn't confidently expect them to be lively.

They were astir with the first streak of daylight. Hardesty and Lone spent the morning exploring for a satisfactory ranch site. So many offered that they despaired of making a choice, until the former came upon a broad park with a clear, sparkling creek running through its middle. There was plenty of pine near at hand with which to build. The afternoon saw the task begun, the sound of the axe ringing cheerily where it was seldom heard.

Three days later saw the long, low, sod-roofed ranch house standing complete. There were clay-packed fireplaces in its two rooms; bunks and tables had been knocked together, horse corrals thrown up beside the creek.

Meanwhile a branding-corral had been built

half a mile away on a convenient flat. Branding the steers was the task next in line; in view of the isolated country through which they had trailed, Lone had advised letting it go rather than run the risk of soreness and the nagging irritation of insects while the brands were healing. Now, however, Hardesty was anxious to get his stock under his own brand. The mark he chose was the 6 Lightning, since there were six in the outfit including Kezzy Sparrow; and the lightning zig-zag was the result of a monogrammed W N, for the White and the Niobrara.

Hardesty was amazed by the speed with which the Texans did their work. Even with the old trail brand to be vented, a single long day sufficed for the branding of the entire herd. Lone said it was because the steers had needed no rounding up.

But once the branding was concluded, the stock was allowed to spread at will through the hills. The work now, as the men settled into it, consisted of riding the ranch boundaries on guard. A constant watch was kept for the Sioux. Hardesty thought it was sheer accident that no band had happened to be on the spot with their arrival. Beyond question one would put in an appearance soon. The punchers had orders to play a waiting game, but to take absolutely no chances whatever. If they were fired on, if the stock was molested in any fashion, they were to act accordingly.

A week passed, two, and nothing happened. Spring insensibly slipped into summer; the steers began to lose their gaunt appearance, to Hardesty's satisfaction. The Texans, at first strung taut in expectation of the unknown, presently relaxed. There was horse-play in the ranch house of an evening; the regular line riding was not the grim business it had started out by being. Even Hardesty allowed himself to be lulled into a sense of security.

One morning Rusty Gallup came riding up to the ranch at a time when he should have been a dozen miles away. He hauled his bronc in with a jerk and the dirt showered. Hardesty, patching a worn bridle inside, reached the door in two long strides.

"What is it?" he rapped out.

One look at Gallup's tense visage was enough. Rusty exclaimed: "Come a-runnin', boss! The blasted redskins've made off with fifty, sixty head!"

Lone, who had come to the door behind Hardesty, let out a bellow. "I knew this was comin', by God!" he swore heatedly. "Things was runnin' too smooth!"

No more time was wasted on words. Racing to the corrals, they got up broncs in a hurry. Kez would have come too, but Hardesty told the boy curtly to stay where he was. Someone had to remain and watch the place.

A moment later, Hardesty, Lone and Rusty set off to the west. They picked up Pony Johnson half an hour later. He saw at once that something was afoot, swinging in with them; a few words sufficed to acquaint him with the facts. They shoved on, while Gallup told what he knew.

He had seen nothing of the raiders, he declared. But on the previous day he had noted some two or three score steers grazing in a wide coulee ten miles from the ranch. There was water nearby; they could not have drifted far; yet today, on reaching the point, he had found not a single head. Suspicious at once, he had circled widely. Soon he had come across the sign of a large, close-packed bunch moving off to the north.

Hardesty nodded his comprehension shortly. There could be little doubt that the cattle were being driven off. It seemed equally plain who were doing it.

Less than an hour took the four to the spot at which the puncher had last spotted sign of the steers. Lone and Hardesty studied the ground briefly. A plainly marked trail led through the hills. They followed it.

Noon came and passed. The country seemed deserted, save for an abundance of small game. Once they saw a timber wolf slink out of sight over a ridge. But Hardesty had known of their presence; a steer or two, pulled down by their agency, had already been reported. Again a band of antelope bounded across the trail and away. It was sufficient to indicate that the steers had passed here long since.

But by mid-afternoon the signs said they were drawing up. Steers will not travel at a fast pace for any length of time; the chief hope of the raiders lay in the possibility that they could cover much ground before their activities were discovered.

An hour later the way led through a gap in the ridges which formed a saddle. Beyond, the rolling plains spread out and away, the tall grass waving in the breeze. Hardesty drew in and pointed an unwavering finger. Some miles ahead the steers could be seen, moving steadily; while around their flanks, urging them to greater efforts, rode half a dozen bronzed warriors.

Hardesty rasped: "We'll make short work of this!" By the set look on the others' faces as they pushed on, they were nothing loath.

Scarcely two minutes passed before the Indians spotted their pursuers. Their efforts to hasten the cattle grew frenzied. Still the punchers drew up. Hardesty had drawn his rifle from the scabbard. At a distance of four hundred yards he threw it to his shoulder and fired.

The others followed suit. "Spread out!" Hardesty cried, waving them to either side. They did as he said, pouring in a hot fire.

The savages were yelling defiance, bunching

on the side of the steers toward their attackers. Hardesty saw that they were Ogalalas, all young braves. They had headed the stock toward low ground, cluttered with willow and alder brush; from the light green sedge grass which grew there, Salem suspected there might be quicksands beyond.

Arrows began to fill the air as the range grew short enough to make their use possible. One whistled past Hardesty's face with an ominous flutter; another struck shivering on Lone's saddle-horn, the splinters flying. Still the pursuers drove in, hot with wrath.

It was too much for the Indians. At the last moment they broke and scattered, seeming to melt amidst the willows. Although wild yells sounded, and Hardesty would have sworn he had seen at least one coppery form topple from the back of a bronc, there was nothing to be found a few moments later, when he reached the spot at which he believed the brave had fallen.

Spread out, and yelling as fiercely as their foes, the Texans were bent on making as clean a sweep of this as possible. But their irregular firing slacked off presently. Despite a superiority in numbers, the Indians had been routed. Such firing of weapons as they had done had been slight.

As for Hardesty, he was thinking more about the steers than anything else. Slowed somewhat by the softness underfoot, they were still shoving toward the low ground; that ominous patch of sedge was not far ahead now.

"Swing 'em!" Hardesty called. "Turn 'em back to higher ground!"

The Texans were well enough versed in the hazards of wild country to comprehend what he had in his mind, and why. Forgetting the Ogalalas, they threw themselves into the task of turning the bunch. It was not easy here in the scattered brush. For a few minutes it looked as though the attempt would be a failure. At last, however, the cattle broke to the side, and ten minutes later were slowing up as they lumbered over safe ground. They were headed back toward their own range.

Lone Benton turned in his saddle to look back, his hard-bitten visage flinty. "Little more uh this, an' the damned copper-colored skunks'll be runnin' all the beef off our stuff, if they don't do nothin' else!" he grumbled testily.

With the reclaiming of the stolen stock, however, Hardesty was feeling easier.

"Might've been worse, Lone," he reminded. "A whole lot worse."

It was true; yet Benton made it doubly clear that he had no more warmth of regard for these hard-riding Ogalala Sioux than for the wily Comanches who had made life difficult for him in the past.

Something better than forty miles had been

covered during the chase. On the way back, Hardesty declared for a swing to the east which, in the course of an hour, brought them to high ground overlooking what he said was Ghost Creek.

"Hey, fer gawsh sakes!" exclaimed Red Tyler a few minutes later. "Don't tell me some of our stuff's drifted way over yere!" He was pointing to a dozen or so steers which could be seen grazing along the creek below.

Hardesty grinned. "No, they're not ours," was all he said; but it was not long before the explanation was made clear. At a widening of the creek bottom could be seen a weathered, sod-roofed log habitation, surrounded by a garden, stock-pens, and the familiar litter of a self-supporting wilderness home.

"Annie Breen's place," Hardesty supplied. Lone stared suspiciously.

"Mean to tell me this place has been here long as it looks for—an' the Injuns leave it alone?"

Hardesty nodded. Ghost Creek, he amplified, had received its name from the fact that years before, a camping band of Sioux had been visited there by an epidemic which had carried off all but its remnants. Ever afterward the Indians had declined to visit the place, declaring it to be haunted. It gave the Breen place a safety which, in this country, could have come about in no other way.

While the punchers held the steers, Hardesty and Lone jogged down there. Before they had fairly arrived they heard a hoarse cry of greeting.

"Well, Hardesty, is it yerself?" exclaimed the woman who stood watching them from the door of her home.

Short and homely, hard-handed as any man, Dublin Annie Breen was inclined to stoutness. Her weathered features were informed with unmistakable shrewdness; and if her stringy hair and far from spotless dress were not pre-possessing, she gave ample evidence of an ability to take care of herself under any circumstances.

Hardesty greeted her heartily, and introduced Lone. "Sorry to hear about Pat——" he added awkwardly, not knowing what to say. Annie's nod was brusque.

"Og'lalas got 'im," she said shortly. But she was scarcely thinking about the past; her whole attention, for some reason, was centered on Lone Benton. Lone squirmed under her regard, acting as if he suddenly didn't know what to do with his hands and feet.

Hardesty came at once to the primary object of his visit, warning the woman of what had happened to him. Annie listened stolidly, shrugging at the end. "The Injuns never bother me," she averred. She appeared so hungry for human company, living alone here as she did, that there was no end to her questions. All the while she eyed Lone appraisingly. At last she shot a sudden query at him:

"Married?"

Flustered, Lone shook his head vehemently. "An' ain't aimin' to be," he hastened to add in a testy mutter. It feazed Dublin Annie none at all. Hardesty was secretly amused by the woman's obvious interest in his companion. They were still talking when a pound of hoofs brought them whirling around.

To Hardesty's surprise, a company of U. S. Cavalry was approaching. It drew up near at hand, and the light-haired, dust-covered Lieutenant who commanded them, young in years but with a forthright practicality of mien, eased himself in the saddle and lifted his hat in greeting.

"Howdy, mam," he said to Annie, who made ribald answer with easy familiarity. Nor did her question delay.

"What ye doin' all the way over yere?"

The Lieutenant explained in a few words. Many Horses' band of Ogalala Sioux, he said, was off the White Clay reservation, wild with liquor and new guns, which they had gotten by some mysterious means. They were raiding the country, burning and killing. The Lieutenant's object was to learn if Annie had any inkling of how the liquor and guns had been smuggled into the country. He glanced keenly and calculatingly at Hardesty as he spoke.

Annie promptly introduced Hardesty. Dodd was the Lieutenant's name. "Don't be thinkin' it's Sale you're lookin' for," she advised him bluntly. "He's an old hand. He was trappin' this country while ye was wonderin' how to git yer corp'ral's stripe!"

Dodd's smile was easy. "You haven't seen any strangers here-abouts? Nobody who might have been smuggling guns and whisky to the Sioux?"

Annie scoffed: "Nah. Nobody ever comes nigh me—"

"Hardesty?" Dodd persisted smoothly.

Hardesty was thinking swiftly. It had been no news to him that the Ogalalas were on the loose. Probably the young braves who had raided his stock were from Many Horses' band. To gain time, he explained what he was doing in the country, and how he had recovered his stolen steers. And all the while the picture of Rafe Perrine hovered in the back of his mind. Should he speak?

In the end he decided not to. He had no definite proof of Perrine's illegal activities. Moreover, there was a personal cast to his feeling about the other which forbade his meddling in Perrine's affairs till the time was ripe.

"Afraid I can't help you, Lieutenant," he said finally, to Lone's surprise. "If I learn anything, I'll let you know."

That also, was the gist of Dublin Annie's answer to the young officer. He did not delay further. A moment later, stiff and military in the saddle, he jogged away at the head of his men.

CHAPTER FIVE

The Cavalry soon disappeared over the low ridge flanking Ghost Creek, going in the direction of Fort Robinson. Dublin Annie Breen gazed that way meditatively for a long moment.

"Reckon I could tell young Dodd a thing or two, if I was a mind to, at that," she mused darkly.

Hardesty caught at the remark. "You mean you know where the Sioux are getting these guns and the whisky?" he queried. Annie's nod was curt.

"Near's I need to," she said. "The white-livered skunks've got a camp over west here, in Spirit Gulch . . ."

"Who are they?" Lone demanded suddenly, with unexpected unction. Annie might not have heard the question, continuing forcefully:

"They better not sashay over yere, if they know what's good for 'em!"

"You know them, then?" Hardesty probed.

Annie did. She admitted as much sulphurously, her dark eyes snapping sparks.

"Who is it?" Hardesty persisted.

"It's Rafe Perrine, dang his black soul!" she burst out. "Him an' that shifty crowd o' no-goods he brought back with him from the Army!"

A shock coursed through Hardesty at this confirmation of his own belief. Lone was bristling as well, glancing around suspiciously as if he expected Perrine to appear at any moment. Still Hardesty hesitated.

"You're dead sure of this?"

"I'm shure, all right!" Annie declared, making plain by her manner that she did not relish having her word doubted.

"Then why didn't you speak up, when Dodd asked if you knew anything definite?"

Watching her face, Hardesty saw a peculiar expression there. He could not identify it with certainty, but there was reluctance in it and more than a trace of chagrin. Dublin Annie flicked him a look.

"Ye'll keep yore trap shut if I tell?" she asked.

"Yes—"

"It's my fri'nd MacKinney," she admitted in a low tone, as if having trouble getting the name out. "I'll never be gettin' him in a jam. Left'nant Dodd is jist young enough that he'd not be takin' such things into consideration."

Hardesty stared.

"You don't mean that you think MacKinney is mixed up with these smugglers?" he exclaimed incredulously.

"No, I don't!" was her tart answer. "There's no thinkin' about it. I know, worse luck!"

Hardesty shook his head. "There must be some mistake—"

Annie exploded sharply. "Mistake is it? Are ye tellin' me what I did or didn't see with me own eyes? . . . I know all about this devil's-nest in Spirit Gulch, if I didn't exactly say as much before. Twice!" she emphasized with out-thrust jaw, "twice I rode up there an saw Colin MacKinney at that camp! . . . Mixed up with these smugglers? He's fetlock deep in their doin's, the fool!"

Hardesty's hackles rose at the words, and his spine went cold at thought of how Glenna would take such a thing. She knew nothing about it, of course; but if it went on, discovery of the truth would be inevitable.

It only served to increase Hardesty's wrath against Perrine. Pretending to think highly of father and daughter, this was how Rafe repaid their friendship. Hardesty had no doubt that if there was anything in Annie's story, it was because Perrine had gained influence over MacKinney in some fashion. It seemed incredible. Then Hardesty remembered what the girl had said about the state of her father's business. It was so bad there was some question whether the trader could go on. That fact alone was enough to afford Perrine leverage.

Hardesty's jaw hardened then.

"I don't believe it!" he said jarringly. "Mac's

too canny; he wouldn't make that kind of a mistake." But even in his own ears it sounded as if he were trying to convince himself, without success.

Annie stiffened.

"Believe it or not; I tell ye I know!" she snorted.

Lone put in a word. "Is Perrine over at this Sperrit Gulch camp now?" he rasped.

She surveyed him coolly. "He is that."

Lone glanced at Hardesty significantly.

"I reckon that's all we need t' know—" He seemed suddenly impatient to pull away.

Hardesty glanced up as if reaching a decision. "Yes," he said slowly. "There's a job waitin' for us! We'll get at it!"

"Hold on!" Annie exclaimed as they swung into the saddle. "What'll ye be after doin' now?"

Hardesty smiled. "You'll hear about it," he predicted with thin satire. Dublin Annie guffawed unexpectedly.

"Give Perrine a crack fer me," she directed harshly. "The dirrty skite!"

But it was not of Perrine that she was thinking as they jogged away. Her glance followed Lone meditatively. "That man kin come back again," she murmured to herself. And then she added, darkly: "He better!"

Hardesty and Benton rejoined the punchers. A glance told that they had something on their minds.

"Let the cows graze," Hardesty told Gallup and Pony Johnson, "and come with us. They're safe here. They'll not drift far."

The Texans looked their surprise. "What's doin'?" Gallup queried.

Hardesty said: "These whisky-peddlin' rifle smugglers. They've got a camp a few miles from here."

It wasn't necessary to add more. They swung away from the herd at a brisk pace, striking across the ridges.

Hardesty was acquainted with Spirit Gulch, a brief gash in the hills walled on one side by rocks, weathered and riven by storms and affording a number of shallow caves. It was an ideal situation for anyone in Perrine's business, for several of the caves made excellent caches.

A mile from the gulch Hardesty drew in. He had been turning things over, and wasted no time now on his plan of action.

"If Annie Breen is right, Perrine will probably have guards out. We don't want any slips."

There was a murmur of agreement, except from Lone, whose grievance against Perrine's crowd scarcely counseled caution. Hardesty went on:

"There's at least six of 'em. That means we'll have to get 'em dead to rights. I don't want any killin'—"

"Hell, let's git on with this!" Lone jerked out, impatience flashing in his gnarled face.

71

"Don't shove on the reins," Hardesty advised him, adding grimly: "You'll probably get all the action you crave before the day's much older!"

With that he turned his bronc and led the way toward the smugglers' camp. For the most part, they were able to stick to the hollows, but now and again it was necessary to cross an opening. Each time Hardesty halted to scan the high ground to the west, but they caught no glimpse, however fleeting, of any sentinel. Twenty minutes brought them within striking distance of Spirit Gulch.

The high rocky wall of the gulch, rising in places to spire-like heights, was on this side. Hardesty studied the rocks a long time before advancing. It was easy for a watching man to melt into the gray monotone of a rock patch; and he was risking no chance of having the quarry warned of their danger too soon.

Dismounting in a shallow coulee, Hardesty motioned for the others to follow suit. "Wait here," he murmured then, starting toward the edge of the gulch with Lone at his heels.

Soon they were amongst the rocks. No yell had sounded; no warning shot sent its echoes crashing through the silence. Crawling on hands and knees, Hardesty made for a point from which he could look down into the gulch. He reached it at last, thrust his head out cautiously. What he saw made his lips thin to a straight line.

Almost directly beneath, in the bottom of the gulch, was a camp. A fire smoldered; several freight wagons stood about; near at hand a number of horses browsed, some of them saddle stock. On a blanket, four men were playing with a greasy pack of cards. A fifth stood looking on, rolling a smoke and making murmurous remarks meant for humor. He appeared to be a little drunk.

It was Rafe Perrine's camp all right. Perrine himself sat on a rock a little distance apart, arms folded and gazing away meditatively as if thinking, unsuspecting.

Annie Breen had been right after all, Hardesty reflected; but there were things about this set-up he did not understand. If Perrine were engaged in smuggling, and there could be little doubt about that, why was he so careless of discovery here? Why, unless he believed his security complete, was there no guard posted?

Hardesty thought the answer might lie in the wagons which stood about. Except for one, which looked like the camp wagon, they were virtually empty. Perhaps Perrine had disposed of his load and had nothing to fear for the present.

But Hardesty had not come here to answer these questions. Elbowing Lone, who craned perilously over the edge, he drew back. Nothing at all was said till they reached a point from which the punchers could be motioned forward. Then:

"We could'a knocked them buzzards off right from where we was," Benton grumbled. "Why not? They deserve it—"

Hardesty said: "We'll do this my way. All I want is to be rid of those gents." To Rusty and Pony he said: "They're there. We'll climb down the rocks and nail 'em cold."

The punchers, their eyes dangerous, were ready for anything. "Lead off," Johnson muttered.

It was some time before Hardesty found a crevice leading down the face of the rocks which afforded cover all the way. He started first, warning the others to silence with a gesture. It was not an easy climb. At the end of ten minutes, Hardesty found himself no more than halfway down. He glanced back. Pony and Rusty were just above; but look as he would, Hardesty saw no sign of Lone. He frowned swiftly.

"What's got into him?" he asked himself. "Does he think he's goin' to take matters in his own hands?"

For a brief space he debated climbing back up the rocks in an effort to locate Benton. Lone might have slipped and wrenched his foot. But Hardesty didn't think so. The other was too old a hand to be caught that way. If he was bent on playing this hand out to suit himself, he would make sure the others didn't locate him till he was ready.

Hardesty shrugged at that, going on. This gully

was steep; he put everything out of his mind except reaching the bottom. They made it at last. Hardesty told the others: "We'll crawl close as we can. But don't make a play till I give the word."

They nodded comprehension.

Slowly, steadily, Hardesty drew up on the camp. At a sudden raising of voices he stole a look, fearing the card game was breaking up; but the men were only shifting around. Rafe Perrine had gotten to his feet and was moving about restlessly.

Hardesty found he could not get as near as he wanted to without crossing an open space. It meant making a dash. Rusty and Pony saw it too. They looked at Hardesty inquiringly. He motioned for them to wait. Then he watched his chance.

The card players he was willing to take a chance on. It was Perrine he had to worry about. Rafe moved about, shooting restless glances as if he sensed something wrong. Hardesty waited for him to turn his back.

Just as he feared his chance would never come, Perrine turned toward the card game and stood motionless. Hardesty started up. It was not more than ten yards to the next patch of rocks; a good seventy-five to the men he wanted to reach. He had scarcely taken three steps before Perrine showed signs of turning this way.

Hardesty would have drawn back, but it was too

late. He froze, the two Texans bursting into full view behind him. Seeing him stop, they attempted to do the same; but Perrine must have caught a flash of movement out of the corner of his eye. He turned swiftly, venting an exclamation. His unerring glance picked out Hardesty and the men with him.

"Look out, boys!"

The cry of warning was barely uttered before Hardesty, making his decision in a twinkling, fired a shot over Perrine's head.

"Don't make a move, any of you!" he called, starting forward with the punchers at his heels.

The renegades paid no attention to Hardesty's words. Perrine wheeled and started to run toward one of the wagons. The men on the blanket scrambled this way and that, rolling over and over as they strove to win to their feet and at the same time learn what threatened.

They halted in their tracks, Perrine included, at the echoing crack of a rifle above their heads. All looked up. High on the rocky wall stood Lone Benton, rifle at shoulder, a look of grim determination on his face.

"Jest make another move!" he invited. "I'm achin' to blast holes in a few of yuh!"

Perrine's visage twisted into lines of hatred and wrath. "What's the meanin' of this, Hardesty?" he exclaimed as the latter came up. Hardesty eyed him implacably.

"You know what it means," was his curt retort. "Get your hands up, Perrine; and don't take a step!"

Rafe exploded violently: "By God, I don't know what it means! By what authority do yuh come bustin' into a peaceable camp this way, shootin' an' raisin' hell?"

"I was satisfied before that you were sellin' whisky and rifles to the Indians," Hardesty told him. "Now I'm sure of it. Do you know what that means?"

Perrine blustered.

"Poppycock! You haven't got a thing on us!" He would have argued further, but Hardesty declined to listen. Telling Gallup and Johnson to watch the captives, he called to Lone that he could come down now.

Benton assented. Without the need for caution, he made the descent swiftly. There was something of the fighting bantam about him as he pushed forward, close to Perrine, looking him in the eye. "Ain't feelin' so funny now, eh?" he rasped.

Hardesty growled: "Forget that. We'll see what we can find in these wagons—"

Perrine warned him to lay off, cursing luridly; but it made no difference. Together, Hardesty and Lone made a thorough examination of the wagons. To their chagrin, they turned up nothing save a cask of whisky, even in the camp wagon, which would constitute evidence of their illicit trade. Lone turned to his companion, perplexed.

"No matter," said Hardesty unemotionally. "They've either disposed of all their stuff or cached it. We'll have a look in the caves."

Ten minutes sufficed to demonstrate that they would find nothing of an incriminating nature there. Perrine wore a hard, satirical smile as they came back.

"Are yuh satisfied now?" he sneered.

"No. But we will be before we get done." Relieving the punchers, Hardesty told them crisply to get all the wagons together.

"Their chuck wagon too?" Pony Johnson queried.

"Yes—"

"What's the idea of that?" Perrine demanded, his features darkening again. His companions cursed under their breath.

"You'll find out."

It did not take long to get the wagons in a pile. Lone struck a match and put it to the brush thrust underneath. Smoke began to curl upward; soon a sheet of flame arose which enveloped the wagons. The punchers had smashed the cask of whisky and poured it over everything, and the alcohol blazed like oil.

Perrine's nostrils were pinched and there were white patches at the corners of his mouth as he watched the destruction of his belongings. He said nothing.

When the last wagon fell into a heap of charred ashes, the wheel-bands curling with the intense heat, Hardesty turned to him.

"Perrine," he said, "that's what happens to gun-runners in this country. Now get up your broncs and pull out—and don't ever come back!"

Relief flooded over the faces of the renegades when they learned their careers were not to be ended here. Yet one of them found the spirit to snarl: "How kin we do that, Hardesty? Yuh burned up all our grub! We'll starve before we git to the Missouri!"

Hardesty turned a hard look on the speaker. He was Pawnee Failes, a hard-bitten Kentuckian. Before Hardesty could speak, however, Lone cried:

"If yuh starve, it's no more'n yuh deserve! Yo're damned lucky we don't plug yore broncs an' set yuh afoot . . . By God, I've a good notion to bore yuh an' be done with it!"

But Hardesty put a stop to that. "Get your horses and go," he directed curtly. "It won't take much to change my mind about turnin' you over to the military!"

Disarmed and helpless, the renegades did as they were told. A few minutes later they started down the gulch, casting black looks over their shoulders. Staring after them, Lone gritted: "I tell yuh, Sale, we're makin' a mistake! We oughta smoke them hombres while we got the chance! They ain't the kind to take orders. Let 'em go like this an' they'll soon be back!"

Hardesty shook his head. "I don't think so," he said at last. He added: "If they do show up again, they'll know what to expect!"

CHAPTER SIX

Winter struck early that year on the northern range. After the long succession of crisp, wine-like fall days, a storm swooped down out of the north and muffled the range. Snow fell a foot deep on the level, and the freezing winds howled around the corners of the log house on the 6 Lightning.

The storm lasted three days. There could be no doubt that it was permanent. More than once Lone Benton stood in the door gazing out gloomily. He had never before seen so much snow at one time in his life.

"I don't like the looks of this," he told Hardesty uneasily. "The steers'll starve in a week's time. Does it happen often up yere?"

Hardesty laughed at him. "Why, this is nothin', Lone," he declared. "Wait till you see a real storm!"

On the following day the skies cleared and the temperature went down. While it was not much below zero, the Texans shivered constantly. The southern plains had never had anything like this to offer.

"Br-r-r!" Rusty Gallup exclaimed, wrapping his coat tighter about him as they made ready to ride the range. "Mama mine! This country was never made fer me! Why, Hardesty, the snow'll never git a chance to melt in this!"

He reckoned without the lingering power of the sun, however. Later that afternoon, when they returned to the ranch, blue from the cold, the ponies breathing plumes of steam in the freezing air, they were nonetheless in better spirits. In a few hours the sun had burned off the snow on the protected sides of the coulees; the stock had been found grazing there contentedly.

Hardesty said smilingly: "You birds are a bunch of sissies. The cows've hardly turned a hair; but you're about ready to turn up yore toes! When you kick the bucket, you'll all have to go to the hot place in self-defense!"

To his surprise, the Texans met his raillery in flushed silence. Ordinarily frank enough concerning their shortcomings, they found nothing whatever funny about the thinness of their skin. Thereafter Hardesty was careful to ignore the subject; but that the Texans suffered intensely in silence was patent. Frosted fingers and ears were a commonplace with them as the winter season settled down in sober earnest and the mercury descended to twenty, thirty, even forty below.

More snow followed speedily. Even Hardesty was ready to admit that so heavy a fall was unusual for October. Yet the steers appeared to stand the weather without difficulty.

But an enemy still more insidious began to attack them presently. That was loneliness. As weeks passed and they saw none but the same familiar faces, day after day, something akin to cabin-fever began to make itself felt. Even Kezzy Sparrow braved the cold for a half day's ride on the range to escape the confinement of the cabin. Hardesty was willing to let him go for the reason that with the snow lying better than two feet deep on the hills, the danger of raiding Indians had disappeared. They were snowed into their winter camps in the valleys of the Rockies, feasting comfortably on pemmican and buffalo jerky, if they were lucky, and would not reappear until spring unlocked the land.

Early in December a warm spell coincided with a storm, with unfortunate results. It rained all day and half the night, turning cold again at dusk. Lone came in the ranch house from seeing to the stock, shaking the rivulets from his slicker. Catching Hardesty's eye, he shook his head soberly.

"It's a-goin' to freeze," he muttered. "Wind's pickin' up too. If this rain don't slack off—" He didn't have to complete the implied prediction of the results.

The others were fully aware of the possibilities. For once they forgot even their boredom in the tension of waiting. A game of seven-up was started, only to languish shortly. Repeatedly one or another of them went to the door, to stare long and anxiously out into the stormy darkness.

It was Pony Johnson who, having stepped outside late in the evening for an armful of firewood, returned with sobriety stamped on his face, his eyes staring.

"It's freezin' fast," he reported. "The hills'll be a glaze of ice by mornin'!"

It was no more than they expected, nor was there anything they could do about it; their very helplessness tightened them up. For his part, Hardesty had never asked himself what would be the outcome of such a situation. The ice covering even the small amount of graze at their command would not mean much to the stock tonight; but tomorrow, when they found their only sustenance locked under a coating of transparent steel, it would be another matter. He tried to remember instances in which an ice storm in this country had been melted off speedily, but could not.

After an hour's worry, without the discovery of a single ray of encouragement, Hardesty got to his feet abruptly. There was decision in his mien.

"Boys," he said, "it's on us and there ain't a thing we can do. We better hit the blankets and get a good night's rest. Tomorrow'll be a hard day."

They knew he was right. Half an hour later only the crackle of the fireplace and an occasional deep sigh from one of the bunks sounded in the cabin. Yet few slept with any soundness. As foreman of the spread, Lone was up and prowling around before the first streaks of steel-gray light stole in at the greased-paper window. Despite the penetrating cold he bustled about, stirring up the fire and getting coffee on.

Hardesty was not far behind him, the others following. Dawn showed them a glittering, steel-clad world. The rain had stopped finally; it was too cold even for snow.

Soon in the saddle, bundled to the ears, they had trouble travelling at all. The knife-like edges of the crust threatened the broncs' legs; on the bare spots it was all they could do to keep their feet. Yet Hardesty saw to it that the condition of the cattle was learned. Bunched in the coulees, the steers pawed disconsolately at the ice sheathing the grass and bellowed their helplessness.

Benton ignored cold and discomfort alike in his concern. "Mebby we could crack the crust an' scrape away enough snow to uncover some feed," he proposed.

It would have been a good suggestion had not the snow stood three feet deep under the ice. Even so they had a try at it; but an hour's work convinced Hardesty that the plan was hopeless. With the tools at their command, they could not have uncovered enough feed to keep more than a score of steers going.

A pale sun emerged in the early afternoon. It

was without sufficient warmth even to start the ice melting in exposed spots. Towards dusk the crew straggled back to the cabin, dejection riding them. All Lone could do, when Hardesty asked him what he thought, was to shake his head dubiously.

As for Hardesty, he began to wonder whether he had tackled more than he could manage in starting a ranch on this storm-battered northern range. In the end, however, his courage prevailed.

"The buffalo stand it," he declared, repeating his argument to Colin MacKinney. "Mostly they stick to the deep mountain valleys, I know; but a lot must get caught in country like this. Who ever heard of winter-killed buffalo?"

"It ain't buffalo we're worryin' about," Rusty Gallup pointed out.

On the following day, to their relief, the sun was stronger. The surface ice began to soften. A close watch was kept on the stock, and a few of the weaker ones had to be tailed up. Late in the afternoon Hardesty found a few steers cropping the exposed tops of grassy tufts. His hopes revived.

Next day saw the melting rivulets more numerous. While some of the steers, browsing on brush, had to be driven to near-by coulees to make sure of them, and Red Tyler reported two cows at least who refused to get to their feet, Hardesty was satisfied. He ordered the two head shot and the beef dressed out, and put the fear of complete and ruthless annihilation away from him.

The following days confirmed his judgment. While the cold did not relax its grip, the snow fell often and plentifully, Hardesty was confident they need not look for a repetition of the ice storm until spring.

Meanwhile he found thoughts multiplying in his mind on which he had not counted. More than once he caught himself picturing Glenna MacKinney. There was an element of frank, insistent hunger in these musings. He wanted to see her again, talk to her, listen to her low-pitched voice that somehow did things to him. And yet, remembering his last reception at MacKinney's Fort, he felt that he could not go there without some adequate excuse. He racked his brains for a reason to get away without satisfactory result.

Matters were at this stand when, on a bright sunshiny morning with the snowfields in the parks a dazzling white, Hardesty was amazed to see approaching the ranch a bundled-up rider whom he did not at first recognize. On the other's arrival, however, he found it to be Dublin Annie Breen. Annie could ride with the hardihood of a man, and wore much the same clothes a man would wear. Just now she had a coonskin cap tied over her head with a scarf, and was wrapped warmly in Pat's buffalo-coat.

"Get down!" Hardesty exclaimed. "Get down

and come in. Is there somethin' we can do for you?"

Lone and the punchers were staying near the cabin this morning; hearing voices, they lost no time in coming to the door. Benton stared at Annie hard for a moment, and his jaw dropped, then snapped shut as if he feared words would emerge before he could stop them. Annie stared at him and the others before replying. When she did so, it was to shake her head.

"It's no favor I've come to ask," she said; "and I'm comfortable where I am—"

Hardesty said: "Going somewheres?"

"I am that," she nodded. A glint appeared in her eyes at the attentive, mystified look on the faces of these men. She chuckled briefly. "Shure, an' ye're like men! Have ye forgotten what day this is?"

"What day is it?"

"Tomorrow," said Annie impressively, "is Christmas. Are ye aimin' to stick yere like bumps on a log?" Herself, she intended going to MacKinney's trading post to spend the holiday with Glenna. "Get yer duds on," she pursued, "an' we'll all go—make it a rale bust. What ye say?" As though by chance, her glance rested on Lone; but if Hardesty's guess was right, there was more of command in it than entreaty.

Benton promptly hedged: "Somebuddy's gotta stay an' watch the place—"

"Fer one day? Nonsense!"

It took little persuasion to make these men see things her way. Isolated as they were, they had completely forgotten the approach of Christmas. Now that it was here, they asked nothing better than a few hours' relaxation.

Accordingly, ten minutes later saw them mounted and riding in the direction of Chadron creek. Apart from his surprise at finding so speedy a solution to his problem, Hardesty was no little pleased. In a few hours he would be watching Glenna, enjoying her company once more. He asked no more of Christmas.

They arrived at the post an hour before dusk, to be greeted by the MacKinneys with grateful warmth. Except for a few friendly Indians, the latter were alone. Glenna lost little time in bustling Annie Breen out of her wraps; yet it was not long before she found opportunity for a word with Hardesty.

"How did your stock weather the ice storm?" she inquired, when they had exchanged a few remarks about themselves.

He told her. "Annie says she lost a steer too— she says it happens every winter, but is no worse than the loss from the big buffalo gray wolves, except when a freak storm hits."

Glenna nodded. "She lost nearly a half of her stock one year. But that is unusual."

He waited for her to say something about Rafe

Perrine, wondering whether the news of what had happened had reached here. But Perrine's name was not mentioned. Hardesty found other reflections to occupy him, however, as the home-made festivities of the Christmas Eve party proceeded and he noted that despite MacKinney's efforts to be agreeable, something was bothering the trader. When someone spoke to him he was cagey and almost morose. Hardesty wondered whether he was remembering the argument at their last meeting. If so, MacKinney made no reference to it.

Despite the trader's depression, it was a gala affair. Seldom were so many people gathered together in this isolated country; the talk at supper was animated.

Hardesty heard wild tales of fortunes in gold wrung from the ground in the Black Hills; legends of crime and lawlessness drifted from there. Glenna said word had arrived late in the fall that the Union Pacific had commenced building that summer in earnest, and would be pushed forward the following spring as soon as weather permitted. There was even talk of bringing Wyoming into the Union as a Territory. But for the most part the girl was quiet, her glance straying again and again to her father. His dark mood plainly troubled her.

Hardesty recalled what Dublin Annie had said about MacKinney's being involved in Perrine's activities. Was that the cause of the trader's uneasiness? Hardesty was glad he had sent Perrine out of the country packing, for Glenna's sake if for no other.

There was a new arrival later in the evening. It was a bearded trapper, drifting up from the Platte country, Gabe Herron by name. He bore his share of fresh news.

"They're sayin' down below the Gov'ment has decided to live up to its last treaty with the Injuns," he announced. "Means the forts on Powder River'll be dismantled, an' the whites moved out . . . That sounds, Sale," he exclaimed to Hardesty, "as if in a year or two we'll be trappin' beaver ag'in. Hey?"

Hardesty shook his head. "I've brought cattle in, Gabe; and brought 'em to stay." Herron snorted.

"Hell yuh have! They'll be movin' you out, too—"

"No they won't." Hardesty was scarcely pleased by the suggestion, but his tone was firm. Annie Breen would also be involved by any such sweeping eviction; she had her say, jerking her square chin down determinedly. For once Lone forgot his diffidence, arguing with her over her causeless apprehensions.

"Sayin' they'll move folks out is one thing," Lone averred stoutly; "an' doin' it is another. They'll never git rid of us as easy as that!"

After supper, with the warmth of an impromptu punch, and urged on by Gabe Herron's fiddling, the party turned into a dance. Chairs and table were pushed out of the way; the trading post assumed an air of activity which it had not known for months. Hardesty danced with Glenna; he was forced to relinquish her, however, before long. Others were waiting.

For some reason, Lone refused to dance at all, but Annie Breen changed his mind; Lone's expression was sour. Hardesty got a grin out of that.

The lack of women proved a drawback till Pony Johnson fastened a blanket about his waist and did his head up in a kerchief. Laughed at, he persisted until the rollicking punchers were arguing for his favor. After that Pony was the belle of the ball.

Except for MacKinney's gloomy countenance hovering on the edge of things, the evening was a great success for the most part until, in a lull in the fiddling, Hardesty held up his hands. "Somebody comin'!" he exclaimed. "Freight wagons pullin' up, sounds like—"

Although he was not amongst those who hastened to the door, he was near when the group there broke up to admit a newcomer. Tall and self-confident, the man walked in. Dead silence greeted him for a moment, and Lone Benton's eyes flashed dangerously. He turned a half-accusing, wholly disgusted look on Hardesty.

The new arrival was Rafe Perrine.

After an awkward pause, MacKinney attempted a halting greeting. Nobody else spoke. Glenna stood arrested, gazing at Perrine with an expression that might have been one of chagrin. As for Rafe, he remained where he had stopped, his eyes, slightly widened, fixed on Hardesty's flinty face.

Hardesty broke the deadlock at last, his words coming flatly: "Perrine, I told you to get out of this country!"

Rafe's bushy brows twitched. Surprised as he might have been by coming face to face with the other so unexpectedly, he was not flustered.

"Somethin' like that," he nodded colorlessly. "It don't mean anything. You didn't get a thing on me; you've got nothin' now, except—" he flicked a significant look in Glenna's direction, "that yuh don't want me around."

"You," Hardesty flung at him ringingly, "are a damned trouble-maker! You've been sellin' rotgut to the Indians since you came back to this country—you supplied Many Horses' bucks with rifles: Spencer .56s, the same kind you're carryin'! I warned you—"

He broke off as an interruption occurred. MacKinney had stepped forward. Whatever of uncertainty there had been about the trader had dropped away from him now. He was grim and stern, his eyes snapping.

"Hold on, Hardesty!" he exclaimed harshly. "Can ye prove all this you're sayin' about Perrine?"

There was dogged insistence in his defense of the other man. Hardesty stared at him for a moment, nonplussed. It was as if MacKinney knew nothing whatever of Perrine's activities and refused to believe in them. Hardesty shook his head.

"I can't prove a thing," he admitted slowly. "But don't make a mistake about this, Mac. I tell you I know!"

The trader was not disposed to argue with him. Warned by the brittle note of danger in Hardesty's voice, he whirled toward the wall suddenly; and when he turned back, a scatter-gun was in his hands, its muzzle menacing the room.

"Believe what ye're a mind to, Hardesty," he rasped, "but don't bring none of your fightin' here! There won't be nothin' happenin' under my roof tonight! D'ye ken that?"

From the moment he had laid eyes on Perrine, Hardesty's fingers had itched to get at the other's throat. Perhaps it had showed in his face. At any rate, MacKinney had forestalled him. The trader had never been one to bluff; he would shoot if he had to.

Perrine gave Hardesty the benefit of his sardonic smile. "Yuh see I've still got a friend or two, in spite of the tales you've spread about me!" he sneered.

Hardesty, the blood pounding in his temples, looked about at the faces of the others. More than a few held his own views where Perrine was concerned. But what hit him hardest was the look on Glenna's face. She was no partisan of Perrine's; but the charges which Hardesty had thrown at him had come as a shock to her. She stared at Hardesty as if she couldn't believe her ears.

"Surely there can be no truth in what you say," she managed steadily, meeting his eye.

On the verge of an imperious reply, Hardesty shrugged. He dared not go too deep into the matter of Perrine's true purpose in this country for fear of involving her father. More than ever now he was convinced that MacKinney stood in mortal fear of what might be said. He darted looks at Perrine, at Annie Breen, at Hardesty, licking dry lips. But the scatter-gun did not waver.

Hardesty turned to Lone. "Get your things on, you and the others," he directed curtly. "We're pullin' out."

About to utter a violent protest, Benton opened his lips—and shut them again as Annie Breen's elbow sank in his ribs. "Okay," he mumbled.

The tension did not relax as they made ready to leave. MacKinney kept a watch on them all. As for Perrine, he rubbed his beefy jaw as if stifling an impulse to laugh. Whatever the thought in his mind, however, he refrained from voicing it.

Shrugging his coat on, Hardesty herded his crew outside and paused in the door. "Good night," he said shortly, and stepped out into the snow.

There were no sounds of revelry from those remaining at the post as they jogged stiffly away, the hoofs of the ponies crunching and squealing on the frosty ground.

CHAPTER SEVEN

If winter had come early, spring was in no haste to make amends. A second ice storm in March, and three weeks later a third, gave the 6 Lightning plenty to do; but their luck held and they pulled through without even the loss of a single head.

But it was not these things which remained in Lone's mind as the snow slowly but surely melted until only huge dirty-white drifts clung to the shadowed shoulders of the coulees. More than once he reverted to the news reported by Gabe Herron, the trapper, during the Christmas party at MacKinney.

"Think there's anythin' in it?" he queried of Hardesty for the third or fourth time. "—This about the Army movin' us all out of the country?"

"We're on land included in the treaty he referred to," Hardesty acknowledged. "But you often hear such moves discussed when nothing comes of it."

"Wal, if Washin'ton does git virtuous," Lone grumbled, "I dunno if there's a thing we kin do 'bout it—"

It was precisely the reflection which weighed heaviest on Hardesty's mind. He knew from past observation that Government rulings on Indian lands could be ruthless in their application, whether to red man or white. And yet, he held stoutly that the army had no right to move out settlers who had been on the ground before their decision was made. Such drastic measures should apply only to newcomers; and if the military posts were to be dismantled, with the consequent loss of protection, it was up to those remaining in the country to take care of themselves. Hardesty himself was willing to take that chance.

The one drawback he saw to the removal of the cavalry from the country was the undeniable slackening of vigilance where the activities of men like Rafe Perrine were concerned. They would have a free hand then, with the result that they would stir up more violence and lawlessness amongst the savages than ever. There might even be a repetition of the bloody raiding which had stained the pages of Kentucky in years gone by.

After what had happened at the trading post, Hardesty no longer doubted Annie Breen's allegations concerning MacKinney's under-cover activities in the smuggling. To one in possession of the key, the trader had showed his hand with fatal certainty in coming to Perrine's defense.

In the old days a trader had been only too careful not to thrust his nose in the business of his customers. MacKinney was too old a hand to have forgotten that teaching. Therefore his support of Perrine in the matter of the smuggling accusation held a definite significance: it was to his own advantage to cover Perrine, keep from him the suspicion of his guilt.

Hardesty pondered long and soberly over the problem. He had no particular sympathy for MacKinney himself. The man must have gone into the thing with his eyes open. But Glenna was another matter. It was for her sake that Hardesty asked himself whether her father should be warned, and if it would do any good.

In the end he decided against such a move. MacKinney would be as jealous of the girl's happiness as any man; he would be sure to resent another's meddling in the matter. Perhaps already he had seen the error of his ways, was trying to get out of the affair, cover up, and put it behind him.

Despite the winter ravages of the big buffalo grays, the spring calf drop on the 6 Lightning was heavy. For a week the men were busy day and night, and when it was over and the calves had safely found their legs, bawling and capering about their mothers, Hardesty felt that prosperity was paying him a visit.

"By golly, we'll have a ranch yet!" Lone exclaimed enthusiastically, surveying his tally-book. "Even sayin' we lost ten percent uh the increase one way or another, it won't be long before we'll have a real herd on our hands!"

The others agreed with him.

99

"Never saw a range where beef critters fatten up so easy," Rusty Gallup averred. "Texas was never like this—"

"Yuh wasn't sayin' that las' January," Kezzy Sparrow twitted him, wiping his hands on his flour-sack apron.

"Wal, Texas was never like that either," the big puncher retorted, "so I ain't said nothin' I can't back up."

Pony Johnson put in: "Wonder how the railroad's comin' along? Them track-layers better hump 'emselves this summer—unless yuh aim to drive to the Black Hills this fall." He was speaking to Hardesty. The latter shook his head.

"There'd probably be high prices there," he said. "But it's all a gamble. If the gold gave out, we might find ourselves in the middle of nowheres with a bunch of stuff we couldn't sell for a dollar a head. And there's always the Indians to consider."

They nodded assent.

"What'll yuh do, then?" Red Tyler queried.

"We'll make our drive to Sidney," Hardesty declared. "The rails may not have reached there; but we can either push on, or find somebody willing to take the stuff off our hands. Next year—" He broke off. It was as yet no certain thing that they would be here a year from now; though Hardesty had determined that if there was any way of managing, he would not be moved out.

His mind was not relieved to any extent by a visit they received early in May. It was in the middle of the day, and Hardesty and the boys were lounging before the ranch house, soaking up the pleasant warmth of the strengthening spring sun while they waited for dinner. Suddenly Pony Johnson got up from squatting on his heels, his far-reaching gaze probing the pines along the north ridge.

"Somebody comin'," he announced.

Indians leaped to the minds of them all, but the tall, lanky cowboy said no. "A redskin wouldn't show hisself so plain till he was ready," he pointed out. "I saw three broncs plain as anythin' in that openin'." He pointed. "You'll see 'em ag'in in a minute."

True to prediction, a few minutes later three horsemen broke from cover and jogged forward. Hardesty saw that they were in Army uniform; and even before the latter arrived, he divined what this visit portended.

The man in the lead was Lieutenant Dodd, from Fort Robinson, whom Hardesty had met the previous fall at Dublin Annie's place on Ghost Creek. His two companions, riding a little to the rear, straight and stiff in the saddle, were troopers.

"How are you, Hardesty—?"

Hardesty nodded. "Howdy, Dodd. Get down."

The Lieutenant did so, removing his hat to

run thin, nervous fingers through his blond hair. His eyes, Hardesty noted, were pale blue, with an opacity common to many men of the stern frontier school.

"Warm," the young officer offered.

Hardesty merely nodded, waiting. He knew it was to this man's advantage to evoke the amenities; but nothing could soften the message he had come to deliver, unless Hardesty was the more mistaken. Dodd appeared desirous of delaying an unpleasant task.

"Have you got enough ranching, yet?" he inquired with a smile.

"Can't say I have."

"But there's plenty of land along the Platte, I should judge, more suited to your purpose—"

"What are you drivin' at?" Hardesty asked flatly. Dodd met his eye momentarily and looked away.

"I don't like to do this, Hardesty," he said at last. "But I have no choice in the matter. Word has come from the East that the Indian lands are to be evacuated by whites, and there's only one reading of that. I suppose you know what it is?"

Hardesty stared at him.

"You mean we've all got to go?" he exclaimed. "MacKinney, Annie Breen, myself?"

Lieutenant Dodd nodded stiffly, but added: "There might be an exception made in MacKinney's case. He has been established here for years; the Sioux depend on him for various necessities—"

Hardesty suppressed a grim smile in which there was little humor. Arms and ammunition, was his interpretation of the "necessities" the savages were most desirous of obtaining.

"What about Rafe Perrine?" he pursued. "Does this new ruling include him?"

Dodd appeared surprised. "Of course. Why not?"

Hardesty shrugged. "A trapper, he calls himself. But if you were basin' your exceptions on the ground of the Indians bein' willin', I expect Perrine would stay."

Lieutenant Dodd scrutinized his face carefully. "Just what do you mean to imply?" he inquired. "Anything in particular—about Perrine, that is?"

Hardesty denied that that was his intention. Dodd let it go without discussion.

"The order to evacuate is effective immediately," he went on. "Of course that doesn't mean we intend to be harsh in the matter—"

Hardesty flushed with anger. Listening keenly, the others began to mutter to themselves. Lone was particularly indignant, glaring at the officer as if he contemplated personal violence.

"You'll be given the necessary time to wind up your affairs here—a week or ten days," Lieutenant Dodd concluded. "I'm sorry, Hardesty, but . . ."

"It's easy to tell me I've got to leave," Hardesty retorted sharply; "but my answer is that I won't, of my own accord. If I go, you'll have to put me off."

Dodd delayed briefly as if digesting this. Then he said in a dry, stiff tone: "All right, Hardesty. I'll report as much to Captain Hanchard."

He swung on his heel and started to mount, when Hardesty halted him.

"Hold on," he said quickly. "There's nothin' personal in this, Lieutenant. Grub-pile'll be ready in just a few minutes. Won't you and your men stay for dinner?"

Dodd hesitated. But a glance at Hardesty's crew told him how awkward such an acceptance would make matters. He said: "Thank you. We've a long trail ahead of us, Hardesty. If it's all the same to you, we'll push on."

"Suit yourself." Hardesty's tone was colorless. He was wondering whether he had said the right thing in answer to Lieutenant Dodd's ultimatum; but a moment's reflection assured him that it made little difference what he said. There could be no resisting the Army, just as there was no changing whatever the Army conceived its duty to be. And yet, as he ran his eye over the fat ridges of this range which he had chosen, rebellion welled in Hardesty afresh. It wasn't fair—

But he dropped that thought almost at once.

What did fairness or unfairness matter in this land without law? A man had by some means to take and hold what he wanted; it had ever been this way on the fringe of the world; it was no different here.

He decided to sleep on the matter before allowing his final opinion to crystallize; but on the following morning he found his chief concern to be how Dublin Annie would take this matter. What would she do, driven from the only home she had known for years? The more he thought of it the more unjust it appeared, and he resolved, before the morning was very old, to ride over and talk with her on the subject.

Starting toward Ghost Creek, he had covered several miles when he spotted a rider going in the same direction. It was Lone. Benton evinced some embarrassment when they met.

"What're you doin' here, off the range?" Hardesty asked.

"Two, three steers drifted over this way some'eres," was the answer. "I was havin' a look for 'em . . . Where you headin'?"

Hardesty told him. Lone nodded. "Looks like there's no steers around," he said. "I'll jest ride 'long with yuh."

They reached Annie's place early in the afternoon. She greeted them wrathfully.

"Heard about these Army doin's, I reckon!" she opened up immediately. "Fine mix-up, that is!

Why, the Injuns wouldn't have this crick o' mine as a gift; an' yet this young brass-buttons, Dodd, says I got to git out! Well, I ain't a-goin'! Any so'jers show up yere, I'll give 'em a piece o' my mind!"

To her surprise, Lone agreed with her emphatically. His sympathies so far ran away with him that he spoke too quickly. "What they think they're doin'," he bristled, "takin' her home away from an old woman?"

Annie shot him a wicked look. "Blast you, Lone Benton; who says I'm an old woman?" she jerked out dangerously.

Lone's jaw dropped. "Not me!" he hastened to disclaim, lamely. "I jest meant they maybe'd do that too, if they had the chance, dang 'em!"

But Annie was scarcely appeased. She regarded him with suspicious disfavor, and whirled on Hardesty. "What're you doin' about this eviction?" she wanted to know.

Hardesty said: "I don't know. I'll ride to Fort Robinson in a few days and see Captain Hanchard. But I don't hold out any hopes of influencing him in the matter."

Much more was said, but this was the gist of their findings. Annie decided that she would ride to Robinson with Hardesty.

Accordingly, several days later, they set out for the little two-company post at the junction of Soldier Creek and White River. They reached the fort that night, and Hardesty was not long in obtaining an audience with the commanding officer.

Captain Hanchard was a stocky, square-jawed man with iron-gray hair at his temples and the mien of a strict disciplinarian. Hardesty concluded to approach him on the soft side if it was possible.

"I hope you've changed your mind about putting all of us folks off our home range," he opened up. Before Hanchard could answer, Annie spoke up, explaining her own situation tartly and making clear that the Sioux had no use for Ghost Creek in any event.

Hanchard heard them out quietly, his face expressionless. At the end he shook his head.

"I wouldn't go so far as to suggest that the creek's being haunted seems strangely appropriate in view of our orders from Washington," he said dryly; "but in any event, the Indian Department has made no provision for such cases." He waited a moment before continuing, and when he did it was plain he was voicing his deliberate intention. "Although I gave Lieutenant Dodd instructions to notify everyone they would have sufficient time, I am going to carry out my own instructions to the letter. They are to remove all whites from the Powder to the Platte; in time, the ruling may even apply to Montana—certainly to the Black Hills. I'm sorry if it inconveniences you, but you are by no means the heaviest losers—"

Before he could go on, Annie burst forth with an angry tirade which it was not probable Captain Hanchard would have taken from anyone else. It affected his decision not at all.

"I'm sorry," he repeated, "but if you people aren't gone in another week, I'll have to send out a company to see to it that you go."

As for Hardesty, he was scarcely surprised; yet the finality of the thing hit him hard. Nearly a year's work and all his hopes were to be swept away at a blow. There would be no more 6 Lightning ranch; the herd would have to be driven east and sold, if possible, to the railroad gangs. It was a bitter pill.

Even so, he was the first to see that it could not be avoided. "There's nothing more to say," he told the irate Annie, urging her to give over. "Captain Hanchard is only obeying orders, and we'll have to take it and like it."

She wilted suddenly, with a tragic look at Lone, who had accompanied them. It made Benton stiffen his back and look fierce, but there was really nothing that he could do.

"Come on, let's git outa here," he mumbled.

Although it was late, they refused the Captain's offer of hospitality. They were swinging into their saddles on the parade ground, when Hardesty paused.

"Hold on," he said as a lone rider pounded toward the fort. "That looks like a courier. He might be carrying some news that would interest us." It was a slim hope, but he was not passing up any chances. "We'll wait and see."

The courier made for the officers' quarters, conferred briefly with a sentry, and was admitted to Captain Hanchard's office. A few minutes later the Captain himself appeared at the door. He waved to Hardesty and the others.

"I just received a dispatch that will interest you, Hardesty," he called, his manner lighter than it had been.

Hardesty and Annie moved forward, even though Lone hung back, muttering suspiciously. The officer said:

"I've got instructions here to relax my stand in the matter of established settlers. It seems this eviction ruling applies chiefly to miners and drifters. The Black Hills will be hit heavy, but according to my reading of this, I am authorized to allow you folks to hold your land as before. Is that better?"

How much better it was might have been gathered from the change of expression on Dublin Annie's face. Her grimness softened and she actually favored Captain Hanchard with an ingratiating smile.

"That's kind of ye, Cap'n," she said. "I'm shore we won't forget it . . . Maybe," she added after a pause, "we'll eat supper with ye an' spend the evenin' yere at the fort after all!"

As for Hardesty, he was bound to admit to himself that the change in the Government ruling had come not a moment too soon.

CHAPTER EIGHT

If there was anyone who resented the most recent change in Washington's policy where the Indian lands were concerned, it was the Sioux themselves. Never able to understand the shifts in Army rulings occasioned by political necessity, they considered it the basest of treachery.

While hundreds of square miles were at stake, it was the loss of the Black Hills which chiefly infuriated the red men. It had been their winter refuge and the home of their gods from time immemorial. According to treaty that land, with its riches of game, was to be restored to them; the Army made repeated promises to empty it of the hordes of miners who had flocked there in defiance of everything. Meanwhile nothing whatever happened. Like a threatening storm on the horizon, the wrath of the tribes gathered.

They were particularly desirous of procuring sufficient arms and ammunition with which to fight the invaders. The trade of the arms smugglers boomed.

Among others, Rafe Perrine was one who found his business thriving. It would have been possible easily to dispose of even more Spencer rifles than he could procure. It wasn't an easy task to get the arms into the country. Alive to the trade, the Army maintained a close watch on the freight constantly being moved in. Only those hardy frontiersmen who knew the back trails were able to get through. Now and then a batch of smuggled weapons was confiscated and destroyed. Perrine was unable to do anything about it, for he could afford to take no chances of his own association with the trade being discovered.

He would have had a hard time of it had it not been for Colin MacKinney. The trader had fallen on hard times several years ago. On his arrival in the country following his discharge from the Confederate Army, Perrine had advanced MacKinney money to carry on. But trade became no better; it was not long before MacKinney found himself not only in debt, but in no position to do anything to change it. Having established his domination over the other man, Perrine coolly proposed a way out. It was to freight Perrine's guns in along with his other supplies. The watch on MacKinney's freight was much less rigid than in most cases; and a few boxes containing Spencer rifles, but marked sugar, for instance, were little liable to molestation.

MacKinney at first refused to listen to such a proposal; but he was in so tight a pinch that he had no way to turn. The first fatal step was taken without awareness of its full significance;

the trader hoped by means of one or two con-signments of guns for Perrine, brought in through his regular trade channels, to crawl out from under his burden of debt; and he succeeded. Meanwhile, Perrine had got the grip on him that he desired. He told MacKinney bluntly what to do, and backed it up with the threat of exposure if he refused. MacKinney gave in.

It was such a trap as the ageing man had never expected to find himself in. He had always been self-reliant; too late he saw that pressure of cir-cumstance had betrayed him. He was in a fever of apprehension lest Glenna should discover his secret. To him, that was far worse than that his defection should be revealed before the world at large.

Perrine read to a hair the hold he had over the other. He fell to spending time at the post. Chiefly he entertained himself by frankly claiming the girl's company. Galling as it was for MacKinney, he knew better than to throw any obstacle in Perrine's way.

As for Glenna, she was at first puzzled, but ended by being deeply troubled. She had no real liking for Perrine; she had never had that; and as time passed, and he persisted in his attentions, there could be no mistaking his intentions.

Nor did he make any effort to disguise his object. Occasionally he proposed rides, hoping to get the girl off by herself. For a week Glenna refused, held back by some vague feeling she could scarcely name. At length, she acquiesced. It was the first and last time, however. Once they were several miles away from the post, Perrine persisted in crowding her close; he tried to capture her hand, to kiss her, to make her listen to his impassioned words. For Glenna it was little short of an ordeal. She had no desire to receive his attentions, yet she feared too frankly to reveal that fact; for there was something darkly tempestuous and head-strong about Perrine. Driven too far, he might easily go to any lengths, taking it for granted that she would eventually forgive him and admit him to her favor.

She wondered why it was, when this man was doing his utmost to make her forget everything else but himself, she should most vividly remember Salem Hardesty's clear-cut features. It was impossible to avoid making a comparison between the two men, and all the advantage lay with Hardesty.

Never by word or act had Hardesty pressed her beyond her will. Though she had more than an inkling of his feelings toward her, she never had had the problem of his impetuosity to deal with. Moreover, Hardesty's quiet demeanor bespoke unmistakable good sense. It was different with Perrine. While Glenna was strongly reluctant to believe what Hardesty had said of him, that he was selling guns and whisky to the Indians, she could not ignore the fact that there was at least a possibility of its truth.

The one thing she found it impossible to understand was why Hardesty had committed himself to words without sufficient proof to back up his accusation. It was not like him. Was it jealousy which had driven him to strike at his rival? Glenna told herself the idea was ridiculous, yet she did not wholly discard it. It made her at the same time both tolerant of, and impatient with, Perrine.

After the one experience, she never went riding with him again.

It did not deter Perrine. He found means to talk to her in private often enough to satisfy himself; and at last he became openly importunate.

"You don't seem to care much for my company," he remarked wryly, one afternoon when she sought to escape him. She darted a look at his face.

"Does it seem so?" She sounded contrite. "It's just that I have a good deal to do—"

He nodded reluctant agreement. "Your father's business *is* gettin' better than it was."

It was true. With the opening of spring, people were moving into the country. There had been an effort to move the miners out of the Black Hills, but it had come to nothing; the gold seekers were flocking in from Sidney, from the Missouri, and even from Montana Territory. They were glad to purchase supplies at MacKinney's Fort even for the high prices the trader charged.

In addition, more ranchers were beginning to drift onto the range. There were four or five outfits besides the 6 Lightning, now, all within a hundred miles of the post.

The normal trade swelled to a point where MacKinney would no longer have found trouble in getting along comfortably. As the clink of hard money in his till became more frequent, he grew to consider his bondage to Perrine in another light.

Perrine was not long in divining that the trader resented their relationship. He became morose when Rafe asked him about expected shipments of rifles, giving the other to understand that he was not to be ordered about with the same freedom as before. Perrine studied him inscrutably on one such occasion, and finally grunted:

"Feelin' your oats, ain't yuh?"

MacKinncy flushed. "What if I am?" he retorted. "Ye've made a pretty good thing o' my good nature—"

"So it's your good nature now, eh?" Perrine sneered. "It was your necessity before, if I remember right!"

"Suppose ye lower your voice," the trader proposed curtly, stealing a quick glance over his shoulder. They were talking in the trade-room, and Glenna might walk in on them at any minute.

Perrine read his thought with ease. "So yo're worried, are yuh? Don't want certain things said. Well, yuh might've remembered that while yuh was wavin' yore nose so high in the air! Yo're takin' near as much money out of this business as I am—"

"Hush, hush, mon!" MacKinney admonished sharply. "Dinna shout! I can hear every word plain; an' there's none of it I don't ken well!"

"Just see to it that yuh remember, then," Perrine told him levelly. But MacKinney was no longer to be beaten down so readily. He met Perrine's stare steadily.

"I'm thinkin' of givin' up the trade," he began stoutly. "This is fair warning, Perrine. Ye'd better do the same—"

Perrine's eyes narrowed. "So that's what's botherin' yuh, is it?" he rasped contemptuously. "Don't worry about me. I'll take care of myself. It's *you* yuh want to be worryin' about!"

There was deep significance in his final words. As bold a face as he strove to put on his defiance, MacKinney shrank in spite of himself.

"What ye mean?" he demanded.

"You know what I mean!" Perrine's mask was wholly off now. A blood-chilling indifference to anything save his own interests showed in the set of his ruthless mouth. "When yuh was down an'

117

out I gave yuh a leg up. Yuh ain't throwin' me down now! You'll go on bringin' the stuff in till I tell yuh to quit. If yuh don't—"

"Ye've as much to lose by talkin' as myself!" MacKinney quavered. "Ye'll no dare go to the law!"

Perrine grinned. "No—but I can go to her." He jerked his head in the direction of the post's living quarters. "How do yuh think she'd like knowin' the truth about yuh?"

MacKinney protested: "Ye'd never do it! Mon, ye stand to lose as much there as I! I know weel enough what your hopes are; ye'd never blacken yerself to the lass!"

"Just kick over the traces," Perrine invited grimly, "an' see whether I would or not!"

For MacKinney, at least, there was little doubt remaining of whether or not he meant what he said. There was nothing for it but to go on as he was doing.

Glenna knew there was something between Perrine and her father. She had no idea what it was. Yet it troubled her. The trader seemed to have changed from his old self, was no longer the good-humored companion she had known and loved. While she loved him no less, she well understood how deep his trouble must be to make him so different.

Once she taxed him with it, but he put her off. Secretly hurt, she was more than ever curious concerning the cause of this difficulty about which he was unwilling to speak.

Again and again she asked herself how Perrine fitted into the puzzle, but without finding any answer. Something told her it could not be because Perrine was so attentive to her. Her father had always encouraged her self-reliance; he knew she could be depended on to take care of herself. Whatever it was, it was something else.

Nor did it appear to be connected in any way with the business. Glenna was aware that financially, her father was in a better position than he had been for a long while. He did not seem resentful of the settlers who were slowly but surely beginning to fill up the country. Despite his lifelong preference for the wild corners of the earth, it was upon the newcomers that his welfare depended.

But for her concern, the girl might never have awakened on the night the first summer shipment of freight for the post arrived. As it was, some time after midnight she lay in her bed and listened to the arrival of the rumbling wagons and the gruff cries of the drivers. She heard her father get up and move about, dressing. A few minutes later he went outside.

She heard him caution a man to be more quiet. His answer was a surly curse; nor did MacKinney's failure to answer sharply and decisively reassure her.

Getting up, she threw a wrap around her shoulders and moved to the window. It was dark outside, but not so dark that she could not follow what went on.

She recognized none of the men out there with her father. A light wagon in which she thought Perrine had occasionally driven to the post for supplies, had met the freight outfits. Under the trader's direction, a number of heavy packing cases was transferred to it from the freight wagons. There was trouble about getting the last case on; at last the men gave it up.

"A'weel," she heard her father sigh. "Leave it here and I'll take care of it." He seemed listless.

The remainder of the freight was unloaded, and the freighters pulled out a little ways along the creek to make camp. Later MacKinney came in and retired once more.

For some reason she could not have named, the whole affair disquieted Glenna. Freight wagons had arrived before at night; in fact it was more common than not; but there had never before been anything mysterious about it.

She was up early in the morning to help with the distribution of the newly arrived supplies. Everything appeared as usual; and yet, one thing she noted particularly: not only was Perrine's light wagon gone, but she could find no trace of the single case which had had to be left behind.

She said nothing, but made her own investigations later, when opportunity afforded. It was not until the following afternoon that she located the missing case. It had been thrust behind a pile of wood in a tumbledown shed some distance from the post.

Glenna stared at it. "BOOTS," was the label stencilled on its side, and it was consigned to her father. Rather than allaying her suspicions, this awakened them. The trader had ordered nothing of that kind, to her certain knowledge. And what could Rafe Perrine want with a large case of them? Had the box been marked "traps," she would have thought no more about the matter.

As it was, she lost no time in hunting up an old axe and knocking off one of the top boards. Her hand, thrust inside, encountered burlap wrappings; but exploring further, she made out hard, metal objects. Face sober, she knocked off a second board, dug into the wrappings. Two minutes later she knew the whole story.

"Rifles!" she breathed. "But why should they be put here, as if hidden?" And then she remembered that this box, unless she was badly mistaken, was the property of Rafe Perrine. More—there flashed in her mind the fact that Salem Hardesty had accused Perrine to his face of secretly smuggling arms to the Indians. No longer could she persuade herself that Hardesty didn't know exactly what he was talking about.

"But Father doesn't know!" she exclaimed. "He can't—"

It was no use, however. The trader knew. His secretiveness, his troubled air; everything pointed to his guilty knowledge. A cold chill settled on Glenna's heart.

"Rafe Perrine!" she managed unsteadily. "It is *he* who is responsible for this—!"

Turning swiftly, she started for the post to find MacKinney. He was in the kitchen, moodily lighting his pipe. Glenna confronted him.

"Father," she began without evasion, "I was awake when the freight wagons came last night. What was it you were transferring to Rafe Perrine's wagon?"

Startled, he stared fixedly for a moment. "Just some supplies he needed," he attempted to put her off. "Grub, traps and the like—"

"It *was* for Perrine?" she demanded flatly.

"Ye-es," he admitted after a delay.

"And what was in the case that had to be left behind—boots, I suppose?"

His face darkened. "What do ye mean?" he countered with some curtness. "What do ye know about that box?"

"I know that it contains the rifles that man is smuggling to the Indians," she came back bravely, "and that you are helping him do it! Oh, Father—" Her voice broke.

MacKinney bristled like a bull terrier. "What!

Rifles, ye say? . . . Are ye tellin' me ye've been nosin' in what don't concern ye?"

But he couldn't carry it off, not under her pleading, reproachful gaze. A few more stumbling words and it all came out; how he had thrown in with Perrine as a last desperate necessity, and how the latter had held him to the traffic ever since under threat of exposure. Even now MacKinney was scarcely impressed by the blackness of his defection; it was the result of her discovery on his daughter that chiefly concerned him.

"Ye won't hate me for it?" he pleaded. "Ye'll no turn against me, lass?"

"Hush," she silenced him hurriedly. "You mustn't speak of such things. Of course I won't—now, less than ever . . . But what are we to do?" she burst out. "This mustn't be allowed to go on! And yet, that—that man has threatened you—"

Never had she expected to loath Rafe Perrine so whole-heartedly as she did at this moment. Had he appeared before her then, there was no telling what she would have said. However, reflection counseled caution, and when Perrine appeared the following day, as ingratiating as ever, she merely avoided him and said nothing.

But the problem she had voiced, of what was to be done, was real and vital to her. She did not dream of allowing events to take their own course. Where she was to turn for help she had no idea whatever, unless—

And then she remembered Hardesty.

What could he do, was the first question she asked herself. The fear that he would be equally helpless, failed altogether to kill her hope. There was always the possibility that he might think of something which had not occurred to her.

Delaying overnight before acting, in the morning Glenna got up her horse and set out for Hardesty's 6 Lightning.

As chance would have it, she met Hardesty himself on the range a mile or two from the ranch house. They came together on a pine-wooded ridge overlooking the White, and he saw at once that something was troubling her deeply.

"What is it?" he greeted, his smile missing for a change. "Are you in trouble, Glenna?"

She forced a smile. "I am, Salem—or rather, Father is," she said. "I was hoping you would know what to do about it." Without softening a single detail, she told him at length of the trader's predicament, and the means by which Rafe Perrine held him to his will.

Hardesty pretended a surprise he did not feel; but his solicitude for this girl, and his wrath against Perrine that she should have had to learn such a thing of her father, were real enough.

"Isn't there some way you can help us?" she put her appeal directly. Hardesty knit his brows.

"Father says Rafe has barely escaped capture several times by the soldiers," she drove on. "He will be sure to involve Father if he is caught . . . There *must* be some way to put a stop to this!"

If there was, Hardesty didn't know what it was, for he had been all over the ground, although Glenna's knowledge of the facts put a different face on the problem. It would bear some thinking over from that angle.

At length Hardesty said: "Say nothing of this to anyone, Glenna. I don't know what it will be, but I'll promise to do something. In the meantime, we mustn't run any unnecessary risks."

She assented gratefully.

"You were right about Perrine before," she said. "I knew you would find a way out—"

"I haven't yet," he warned. "But my experience has been that there are few problems which haven't a solution somewhere. The solution to this one must be found . . . Go back to the post, Glenna, and try to act as though nothing were wrong. I'll ride a ways with you. And don't worry about your father. Given time, I can promise that I'll do something."

The look of faith in her eyes said that that promise was all she asked of him.

CHAPTER NINE

When Hardesty took leave of Glenna and rode back to the 6 Lightning, he was in a brown study. One question bulked large in his thoughts: what could he do? He could not disguise from himself the fact that he had made his promises largely for the sake of the girl's peace of mind. As for saving her father, there appeared no ready solution short of rubbing Rafe Perrine out.

Lone Benton met him at the corrals. Noting Hardesty's sober preoccupation, he asked what was wrong. Lone knew all there was to know about Perrine; Hardesty told him briefly and frankly what Glenna had had to say.

"Perrine's got 'em where the hair is short," he wound up. "I don't know what to do."

Lone liked the business no better than he did. "A rope's what them dang renegades need!" he responded forcefully. "Why can't we round 'em up an' git it over with? There ain't no law out yere to worry yuh; anybody that found out 'bout it would be only too ready to thank us—"

Hardesty shook his head. He wanted time to think the matter over more fully. Going into the cabin, he sank into a raw-hided chair and fell to pondering deeply. The minutes passed, and he did not so much as change position. However, a knock at the open door some time later was sufficiently surprising to arouse him from his abstraction.

Before Hardesty had time to get to his feet, a bulky figure darkened the door and a man stepped in. Raising slowly, Hardesty stared his amazement. It was Rafe Perrine.

Hardesty was the first to speak. "What are you doin' here?" he demanded hoarsely. But even as he voiced the question, he knew. Perrine had witnessed his meeting with Glenna; he must have divined the girl's reason for coming to Hardesty. This, then, was his answer.

His swarthy cheeks were cold, expressionless. He said: "I'm savin' yuh the trouble of huntin' me up, Hardesty." There was flat challenge in the words, and he pushed it further. "I know what yuh got in yore mind . . . Forget it!"

Salem's jaws corded. "I warned you, Perrine," he rasped thinly. Rafe's laugh was deliberately insulting.

"I know how yuh feel about the girl," he retorted easily. "For your sake it's rather unfortunate—"

Hardesty's face flamed with the hatred and fury he had all he could do to master.

"What do you mean?" he blazed. Perrine met his look with one as dangerous.

"You'll keep yore hands out of my business,

if yuh know what's good for yuh," he assured, adding: "Make a move, an' I'll drag MacKinney down with me!"

Hardesty swept prudence aside in a flash. There was no way of curbing any longer the rage he felt against this man. Perrine was a dozen feet away, standing in the middle of the floor. Hardesty sprang toward him.

With a lightning-swift movement, Perrine drew his gun. Its muzzle trained unwaveringly at Hardesty's middle.

"No yuh don't!" Rafe grated. "Take another step, Hardesty, an' I'll blast yuh to hell! . . . Maybe I will anyway," he continued with rising anger. "By God, you've had yore nose in my affairs too long as it is."

Hardesty knew only too well how thin was the thread on which his life hung. Since their meeting in Spirit Gulch, Rafe had been waiting for this moment. He would not be likely to let it slip through his fingers. Hardesty's thoughts moved swiftly. In an effort to distract the other, his glance switched to the door.

"Don't shoot, Lone!" he exclaimed. "I want to square accounts with him first—"

Perrine's lips split in a sardonic grin. He did not turn his head.

"It won't work, Hardesty," he taunted. "I got wise to that worn-out trick a long time ago!"

To the surprise of them both, a shot crashed

unwarningly. Perrine jerked as a slug grazed his gun-arm and he dropped the Colt. Lone Benton stood in the door, his weapon ready.

"Sometimes yuh know too much, Perrine," he jerked out with a wolfish grin. "Here's once where yuh made a big mistake." He nodded to Hardesty. "Okay, Sale—I'll see to it there ain't no more dirty work!"

Recovering from his surprise as quickly as Perrine, Hardesty moved forward. He was in no mood for half measures now. In another minute this man would have shot him down without compunction. But there was already more than enough chalked up to his credit to have damned him.

Keeping a wary eye on Hardesty, Rafe was feeling about with his toe for his fallen gun. Hardesty put an end to that by letting loose a blow which Perrine narrowly avoided. Bellowing his protest, the latter came back with a wild swing. Then they were at it, toe to toe; trading blows which came up from the floor, and jarred a man heavily when they landed right.

Perrine's wound was little more than a scratch. It did not interfere with his fighting. And his failure to kill Hardesty outright in the moment he had the other under his gun, seemed to infuriate him. He made rush after rush, as if he would rectify the omission with his fists.

Hardesty asked for nothing better. While

Perrine's raking punches left a spreading ache on his ribs and brought the blood to his face, he found a deep satisfaction in hitting Rafe with everything he had. There was no cleanness about the big fellow's fighting. When a short-arm jolt of Hardesty's swept him off his feet and to the floor, he snatched up a chair as he came to his knees and hurled it. Hardesty covered his head with an arm; the chair broke as he staggered back.

Perrine was on him with a bellow. They grappled, went down on the rammed dirt floor with a shock; Hardesty underneath. He was struggling desperately now. Biting his mustache fiercely, Lone wanted to rush in, pull off Perrine and hurl him into a corner; but he restrained himself.

With a heave, just as Perrine's knee threatened his stomach, Hardesty flung his antagonist over his head. Perrine landed on head and shoulders. They gained their feet in a twinkling, and closed once more.

Right and left, they exchanged murderous jabs; the blows were coming more slowly now. Both were feeling the drag of great effort. Rafe rushed in suddenly, seemed to stumble, and grappled. Avoiding a wild rabbit-punch, Hardesty sledged Perrine's midriff savagely. The latter lurched, caught himself and aimed a kick. For the moment his defenses were down. Stepping close, Hardesty threw in a jolt to the jaw like a lightning-bolt.

The blow sounded like the flat of an axe against beef.

Perrine dropped. Hardesty stood over him, wavering, his breath coming in gasps.

"Watch out, Sale!" Lone warned. "He's a dirty sidewinder fer tricks!"

But Rafe was playing no more tricks at present. When Hardesty jerked him to his feet, he staggered and would have fallen but for the other's support. His face was cut and swollen; all the belligerence had poured out of him.

Still he made futile efforts to strike at his enemy. Whatever he was, there wasn't a yellow bone in his body. Hardesty slapped him into submission, a look of distaste and contempt on his grim visage.

"Stand aside, Sale!" Lone begged. "Lemme shoot the polecat! Yo're done with him—there ain't a lick o' sense in allowin' him to go on livin'!"

Hardesty thrust in between decisively, however. "Forget it!" he advised sharply. "Whatever Perrine has done to us all, he won't force us to carry that load!"

Perrine was not beyond understanding what passed. "Make away with me, an' it'll go hard with yuh!" he bluffed, mumbling through broken lips. Thrusting him back, Hardesty eyed him perplexedly.

"I'm warnin' you a second time to get out of

the country, Perrine!" he said curtly. "I won't do it a third time! . . . I'm goin' to Fort Robinson tomorrow with the facts. That'll give you twenty-four hours to pull your freight and distance pursuit. If you don't, it'll be curtains for you!"

Rafe flared with a brief return of defiance. "You'll do nothin' of the kind," he exclaimed. "Give me away an' it'll mean MacKinney goes with me—"

"MacKinney's ahead of you," was the brusque answer. "He's ready to talk, if need be to get rid of you, and take his medicine. It'll be your finish, I tell you!"

Perrine scoffed. His venom was bitter. "All bluff!" he insisted. "Yuh don't dare make such a play—the girl'll never look at yuh again!"

Hardesty gritted his teeth. It was impossible to beat the malevolence out of this man's twisted nature. He said: "You take a chance on what I don't dare do, and see what happens! In the meantime, get off my ranch; it's beginnin' to smell bad around here!"

Taking Perrine by the shoulders, he whirled him toward the door and flung him out. Big as he was, Rafe's strength was so far gone that he measured his length in the dust. He picked himself up cursing.

"I'll settle with yuh for this!" he raged. A foot shorter, but every bit as stout of heart, Lone thrust close and shoved his jaw out.

132

"Easy with yore threats, Perrine," he suggested thinly, "or you'll never get boot in yore stirrups again! I ain't as forbearin' of locoed coyotes as Hardesty is!"

Muttering under his breath, Perrine flung away toward his bronc. They let him drag himself into the saddle the best way he could. Jogging away from the ranch, he looked a thoroughly whipped man. But there was fierceness in the slit-eyed glance he tossed over his shoulder from the first fringe of pines.

"Yo're makin' a big mistake, Hardesty," he muttered to himself. "But it's all right with me! I'll find a way to fix yore clock before I get done!"

After some minutes of brooding reflection, he continued. "My real danger is old MacKinney. Without his mealy chatter they won't have a thing on me. I've got to stop his mouth in a hurry!"

How it was to be done he did not immediately see; but he rode on his way, pondering the problem. Nor was it long before an expression of sinister satisfaction at the direction of his thoughts began to appear on his face.

Hardesty had not been bluffing in telling Perrine what he intended to do. He had long since come to the conclusion that drastic measures were necessary to solve the tangle involving Colin MacKinney. Accordingly, the following morning saw him in the saddle early and on his way to Fort Robinson to carry out his intention of laying the facts before Captain Hanchard.

There appeared little hope that MacKinney could be spared the price of his misstep, particularly if Perrine were apprehended. But the extenuating circumstance that Rafe had got the trader in a jam and was forcing him to aid in the smuggling of contraband goods, offered the hope of leniency at least. Hard as even that would be on Glenna, it was better than continued bondage.

Hardesty found it impossible to get the girl out of his thoughts as he neared MacKinney's Fort on his way to the military post. He wondered how she would take what he was doing; whether she would hate him for the means he found to deal with Perrine.

There were a number of broncs standing outside when he came within sight of the trading post. To his mind there was a vague air of trouble about the place. No one was in sight. Dropping his intention to pass the place without stopping, he swung off his pony and stepped to the door.

Glenna was inside. She looked up, and he saw at once the marks of grief in her face.

"What is it?" he queried quickly.

"It's Father," she managed in a suppressed voice. "He's dead—"

"Dead?" He stared at her blankly. "When did it happen?"

"This morning."

"How, Glenna?"

"It was—an accident," she told him. "Rafe Perrine and two of his friends were here when an Indian came in. Crow Feather, it was. I think he was drunk . . ."

Mention of Perrine warned Hardesty what to expect. He interrupted: "Who were the pair with Perrine?"

"Abe Slater and a man called Pawnee—"

Hardesty nodded. He remembered Pawnee Failes.

"What did they do?"

"It was Crow Feather who began it. He demanded whisky of Father." She was fighting her shock bravely. "Rafe spoke to the Indian. He told him to go outside and keep quiet. Suddenly, Crow Feather turned on Rafe. He had a knife. He was going to stab him—"

"And then?"

"Abe Slater pulled his gun. I think he meant to protect Perrine. He fired at the Indian. But the shot went wild. I heard Father cry out. Before I could reach him, he fell!" She struggled with her memory of that terrible moment. After a moment she concluded: "The bullet struck him in the chest. He was—dead."

Hardesty's first impulse was to comfort her. Instead, he held himself with a hard grip. He was under no illusions as to the "accident" which had happened. MacKinney's murder had been cold-bloodedly planned and carried through. It was Perrine's answer to Hardesty's final warning. The latter demanded:

"Where is Perrine now?"

"He and the others left, it must be an hour ago."

Grim-faced, Hardesty whirled and started for the door, only to pause. "This Indian—Crow Feather? What became of him?"

"He left at the same time. I think Father's death subdued him, for he said no more about whisky. Perrine kicked him out of the building, warned him not to come back."

"Oh, he did?" Hardesty caught at that. "Was Crow Feather an Ogalala?"

"No, an Uncpapa. His people were camping a few miles down the river."

It was enough for Hardesty. Promising to be back soon, he made for his horse, mounted, and headed down the Chadron toward White River. He knew the favorite camping places of the summer bands. Soon he reached the camp of Walking Bear, the Uncpapa chief. It was an interesting scene, here in the midst of this wild setting; but Hardesty made his way without pause to the tepee of the chief and asked to see him.

Walking Bear, a dignified, imperious old fellow, knew him of old. He was not surprised when Hardesty stated his errand bluntly. Did Walking

Bear know that his old friend, MacKinney the trader, was dead? One of his warriors, Crow Feather, had seen it happen. The soldiers were going to look into it. Hardesty wanted Crow Feather to return with him to the trading post and answer a few questions.

At the mention of soldiers, Walking Bear was not inclined to be haughty. He deliberated for effect, then announced that he would see if Crow Feather was in the camp.

The latter was. He eyed Hardesty sullenly on being brought before the chief, but admitted that he had been present at MacKinney's death and knew what had happened. He consented to return to the post with Hardesty when directed sternly by the chief to do so.

The two rode away from the camp in ominous silence. No signs of activity appeared as yet, but Hardesty well knew that within an hour, this camp would have disappeared like mist on the river before the morning sun. Crow Feather no doubt was expected to take care of himself as best he could.

Whatever he had been a couple of hours ago, the Indian was stone sober now. He eyed Hardesty sidewise bleakly and apparently would have been only too glad to sink a yard of arrow-wood into him given the opportunity.

Glenna watched them approach from the door of the post. When the brave dismounted,

Hardesty grasped him by the arm and guided him inside. Crow Feather darted nervous looks about, then decided to bluff it through.

"Is this the man?" Hardesty asked Glenna. She could only nod. Hardesty rounded on the savage.

"Crow Feather, you saw MacKinney killed. You helped do it," he jerked out. "Why?"

The Indian's snake-like eyes narrowed. He was like a hunted animal, and would have made a break had there been a ghost of a chance. There was none. He muttered uneasily:

"I know no-t'ing. Let me go!"

Hardesty only moved closer.

"Crow Feather, we know what you were doing. We are not saying you are to blame. Tell the truth and it will be forgotten . . . Who told you to start a fight in here?"

The Indian squirmed inwardly, caught by that stern glance like an insect on a pin.

"No-body," he grunted vehemently. "I want drink. MacKeeny no give. Rafe Perrine tell me get out. I no like. Slat-air shoot. He miss me. Mac-Keeny—"

"I know," Hardesty cut him off. "That's what happened. You did not kill MacKinney . . . But who told you to ask for whisky?"

Crow Feather would have denied that anyone did, but Hardesty gave him no chance. "Was it Perrine?"

The Indian wavered.

"You no geev me to soldiers?" he said. Hardesty and the girl exchanged glances.

"No. All we want is the truth."

Crow Feather grunted his relief. "It was Perrine. He tell me come in, start fight. He do it."

"Then he wanted MacKinney killed, Crow Feather?" Hardesty awaited the answer tensely. The brave nodded stolidly.

"What did Perrine promise you for doing this?"

"Wheesky," was the unemotional response. "Wheesky and gun." A new thought struck Crow Feather hard. "You no stop Per-rine from geev me?" he demanded anxiously.

Hardesty rasped: "That's enough! Get out of here, you treacherous dog, before I finish you!" His look was so threatening that the Indian fell back. He knew he would get no more satisfaction here. With a stealthy look about, he glided to the door. A moment later he was gone.

Hardesty and Glenna were gazing at each other in the portentous silence. Each knew the riddle of the trader's death had been solved, and solved correctly.

"The Indian," Hardesty rasped jarringly, "was one detail that Perrine overlooked!"

The girl's face was pinched and white. "To think that I was willing to believe Father's death was an accident!" she whispered. "You are right about Rafe Perrine, Salem. You were always right about him!"

Hardesty nodded curtly.

"Right now, my first job will be to hunt Perrine up," he declared. "I should have done it before; but this time I'll call him and Pawnee Failes and Abe Slater to account in short order!"

He was mistaken about this, however. He admitted as much when, three days later, he had visited every place where the three men might possibly be found, without locating a trace of them. Rafe Perrine and his men might have taken wing, so completely had they disappeared.

CHAPTER TEN

Admitting to himself that Perrine had escaped him in the end was a bitter pill for Hardesty. On his return to the trading post he told Glenna just what had happened at his ranch when Rafe appeared there. The girl showed no inclination to hold him to account.

"But what will you do?" Hardesty queried. "You'll be all alone now," he reminded.

She did not appear to consider the matter a serious problem. "I'll stay on here and run the business, I suppose," she said. "There is nothing else I can do."

The thought flashed in Hardesty's mind to ask her to marry him. He would have asked nothing better of fate, and in that way Glenna's protection would have been assured. But he put the hope from him. Marriage was the last thing she would care to consider with her father scarcely cold in his grave.

Hardesty would have worried considerably over her welfare except for several things that happened that summer. In June a stage-line began to run through on its way north to the gold camps. The permanence of Deadwood, that roaring city in the Black Hills, had become assured; it was the Sidney-Deadwood stage which made MacKinney's Fort a rest-stop on its way.

Not long after, a man of some enterprise stopped off at the trading post and remained for several days, watching the flow of miners, settlers and cowmen which converged on the place. His name was Henderson, and on his taking leave at the end of the third day, it was with the promise that he would soon be back. He was as good as his word. When he reappeared a fortnight later, it was in charge of several freight outfits loaded with raw, fresh-cut pine timber from the saw-mills in the Black Hills. He had several carpenters with him. When the clatter of hammers and rasp of saws ceased, a jerry-built structure had risen across the stage-trail from the trading post. Although the saloon which occupied most of its ground floor was the chief reason for its existence, the place was dignified with the name of Henderson's Hotel.

Thereafter, there were always a few white men around on whom Glenna could depend at need. Hardesty made it a point to meet Henderson, and satisfied himself that the man would allow none of the wild carousing so common to frontier outposts. Henderson as a matter of fact had hopes for the growth of MacKinney, as the place was beginning to be called, into a respectable, civilized community.

Meanwhile, it was a matter of no little interest to Hardesty himself that more ranchers continued to drift into the country from the south. Some started a shoestring outfit; others were more pretentious. For his part, Lone Benton was not sure he liked the change.

"Little more, an' this range'll be as cluttered up with two-bit spreads as Texas," he grumbled. "We'll be forced to shove off fer Wyomin' to give ourselves elbow-room!"

He did not mean it, however. All his apprehension was occasioned by the fact that incoming ranchers were showing undue interest in the 6 Lightning range. It was no uncommon thing now to meet with strange punchers, drifting that way occasionally on some errand of their own.

Hardesty saw to it that he made the acquaintance of the incoming cowmen. They were all a little suspicious of one another, and there was no attempt at order in the manner of their settlement. Good range was speedily grabbed up wherever it was found; and the incertitude of priority was the occasion for several violent clashes. One outfit of four men was nearly wiped out in a shooting fray one night in Henderson's saloon; the single survivor rode away the same night in haste, and forgot to come back.

Still the talk was all of expansion. Riches poured out of the Black Hills in a golden stream; men passed through MacKinney on their way there by every stage. The Union Pacific had reached Sidney, seventy odd miles to the south;

freight outfits were busy, transporting supplies north from the end of track.

One day at dinner Pony Johnson came out with an announcement which made Hardesty sit up. It was to the effect that Pawnee Failes had returned and started a small spread a few miles south of the 6 Lightning.

"Failes? Are you sure of that?" Hardesty demanded of the tall puncher.

Johnson was. "I run into Jack Naylor, another of Rafe Perrine's old cronies, an' invited him to give an account of himself. Said he was workin' fer Pawnee—"

"What's Failes's brand?"

"Diamond Cross," Pony supplied. He illustrated. Across the table, Lone grunted:

"Double-Cross'd be a better name fer it!" He turned to Hardesty. "Yuh payin' Pawnee a visit? He was there at the post when MacKinney was rubbed out," he reminded.

Hardesty shrugged. "What's the good? I couldn't get anything out of Failes. I know all I need to know, anyway. It's Perrine I crave to meet up with."

During the days that followed, Hardesty asked himself what Failes's object could be in returning to this range. If he had broken off his connections with Rafe Perrine, that would be a sufficient reason for his seeking some legitimate means of livelihood; for with the country filling

144

up as it was, smuggling arms to the Indians was no longer an easy, profitable business. Although an occasional act of violence attributed to them was reported, the Sioux were becoming scarce hereabouts, most of them drifting north and west to wilder country.

If Hardesty wondered whether Pawnee would give him any trouble, or would be willing to let bygones be bygones, however, he soon had his answer. One morning as he and the boys were making ready for the day's work, Rusty Gallup, who had spent the night in the saddle, came racing into the yard on a lathered bronc.

"Hit leather, boys!" he cried. "They're crowdin' us now!"

Hardesty grabbed his bridle. "Hold on, here; tell your story," he jerked out.

It was soon told. Some five hundred head of steers had been shoved onto 6 Lightning range, a dozen miles down the Niobrara, Gallup declared. They were Diamond Cross stuff. There were a number of men with them. Rusty said:

"I warned one of 'em he was on our range. He told me to go to hell. Jack Naylor, it was—"

"Whyn't yuh blast the coyote?" Lone Benton burst out. The puncher eyed him shrewdly.

"That would'a been sense, wouldn't it—with his crowd right there with 'im? They'd made short work uh me, an' I knowed it!"

Hardesty nodded.

145

"Rusty did right," he said. "He wouldn't be any good to us dead. We'll get over there right away. They'll be waitin' for us!"

Hardesty, Lone, Pony Johnson and Red Tyler started at once. Delaying long enough to catch up a fresh mount, Gallup caught up. They were soon within sight of the Niobrara. Occasional sand hills gleamed in the sun above the white clay cliffs across the stream. Rusty said the invaders were still several miles down the river.

Their first warning as they pushed through the scattered pines was a rifle-shot. It failed to halt them. Bursting through the trees a few moments later, they saw the marksman, alone, racing across open range toward the herd of steers which had already begun to spread out. Hardesty went hot at the sight. There was little use trying to overhaul the fleeing puncher.

"Swing north," Hardesty called to his men. "We'll bunch this Diamond Cross stuff and shove it back into the rough!"

They did as he said. Pawnee Failes's herd had not had time to scatter widely. Once or twice they caught a glimpse of a Diamond Cross puncher, but each time he was heading the other way in a hurry. Apparently there was to be no determined resistance.

Under Hardesty's direction, the steers were headed back toward the river. It was not very deep. They plunged in, splashing and bellowing, and waded across. A break occurred in the white cliffs here. It was the way the steers had been driven down to the stream. Hardesty saw them headed back the way they had come, and made sure they were shoved far enough so that they would not drift back. Then he rode on ahead and showed himself on a high swell. He was not surprised when, a few minutes later, a horseman appeared and jogged toward him. It was Pawnee Failes.

"What's the idear of foggin' my steers all over the map, Hardesty?" he opened up belligerently.

Hardesty avoided argument, retorting coolly and quietly: "North of the river is 6 Lightning range, Failes. Stay off!"

Pawnee blustered: "The hell yuh say! I got as much right there as you!" He would have had more to say, but Hardesty cut him off.

"If you value your stock, keep it away. That's a final word." Turning his bronc, he jogged back toward his own range. Pawnee glared after him, and burst into bitter invective; but he made no move to go for the gun Hardesty knew he was itching to use.

Lone Benton came jogging up a moment later to join Hardesty. "Yo're bein' mighty easy on these hombres, Sale," he warned. "It won't come to no good. If I was you—"

"But you ain't," Hardesty smiled. He added:

"Pawnee knows where he stands. He won't make another mistake in a hurry."

A few days later, Red Tyler brought back from MacKinney the story of another attempt to jump preëmpted range. This time there was a gun fight in which one man was killed and several wounded. The ranchers were getting wrathy, Tyler reported. There had been talk of running several renegade cowmen out of the country.

That very day Pony Johnson was fired on from ambush as he rode the range. The slug had gashed his ribs, but did not prevent him from giving chase to the would-be assassin. The latter soon outdistanced pursuit, fleeing south across the Niobrara, where Pony had lost his sign in the sand hills.

"See who it was?" Hardesty demanded.

"No," the lanky Texan shook his head. "But I don't need that to tell me what I wanta know!"

Hardesty himself had little doubt that one of Pawnee Failes's crowd had been responsible. Common sense warned him against taking the law into his own hands, however. With so many rough men in the country, there was no telling where an outbreak would end.

Yet he was not minded to pass the condition over without taking action. The following morning he and Lone headed for MacKinney with a definite purpose in view. Hardesty found Glenna situated comfortably and getting along well. Her business was growing almost daily and she had nothing whatever to complain of. And yet, there was a shadowy sadness about her face. She could not forget that her father had been needlessly robbed of perhaps many years—the only peaceful period life had ever offered him.

At Henderson's, Hardesty met Gabe Kyle and Mart Pincher, two ranchers who had been in the country since the previous fall. They listened approvingly to his proposal of a meeting, but thought that all the cowmen who would consent to attend should be notified. This coincided with Hardesty's opinion exactly.

Accordingly, messengers were sent to the various ranches with word to gather for a meeting with a view to the best advantage of them all. It was the first attempt at lawful organization in western Nebraska; and with an eye to future business, Henderson took advantage of the opportunity to offer the use of his hotel office for the affair.

It was accepted. The meeting was set for three days hence, but before the day was out, ranchers willing and eager to participate began to put in an appearance. Others followed.

There were fifteen men who crowded into the little room when the time came. All were rough and weathered, young for the most part, though a few graying heads showed in the gathering. All were outspoken, plain in their opinions; but none had any idea how such an affair should be conducted till Hardesty took hold.

Pawnee Failes was among them. At first contemptuous of the business, he had decided to ignore the summons, but had changed his mind on learning that every other cowman of any importance in the country expected to attend.

"I'm right glad to see so many of you here," Hardesty opened up. "It won't do to overlook the seriousness of what brings us together today. There's no law on this range except that at Fort Robinson—which is practically useless where our troubles are concerned. So it's up to us to make our own law.

"For one thing, a stop has got to be put to this range-grabbing that's been going on. Lives have already been lost, and more will be, unless we take a firm stand. That's what we're here for. We're goin' to decide on regulations that must be followed for the good of all."

It was the beginning of a stormy but hard-headed session. Few of these men could lay a valid claim to the land they used as range; for that reason the arguments concerning open range and water-rights which had come down from biblical times, were raked over and threshed out. In a fenceless land, there was the matter of drifting stock to be settled; and a general round-up was planned for the fall.

"You all know what this means," Hardesty

pointed out, when the matter was settled. "There's bound to be differences over stray calves next spring. Why not guard against it before blood is spilled?"

"How'll yuh do that?" a gruff voice demanded.

"By reaching an agreement not to brand mavericks under any circumstances before a certain date," Hardesty responded.

It was discussed warmly, but in the end the plan was accepted. Even Pawnee Failes was forced to agree to the ruling, little as he liked it. After more business, largely concerned with the fall round-up, the meeting dissolved.

Glenna's approval when she learned what had been accomplished was hearty. "It's the first step toward real law and order, Salem," she said.

If there flashed in his mind remembrance of the fact that all law and order movements came about as a result of a condition requiring such an answer, he said nothing. It would not do to ask for trouble. But in the back of his head lurked the certainty that trouble would make its own uninvited appearance before long. Nor was he mistaken. Less than a week after the cattlemen's meeting, Kezzy Sparrow returned from a supply-purchasing trip to MacKinney with word that several cases of rustling had been reported over west. "Gabe Kyle lost a dozen head," Kezzy announced, "an' Ep Granger thinks he's been hit even harder. He ain't shore."

Hardesty's nod was short. "I expected somethin' of the sort. It means we'll have to keep a closer watch of our own stuff from now on."

However, they could not watch so closely that the rustlers were unable to get into 6 Lightning beef. Lone Benton came pounding in one afternoon two days later with the discovery.

"They've run off eighteen or twenty head!" he told Hardesty heatedly. "I come acrost the sign where they crossed the White! They're headin' north an' not wastin' no time about it; they must've had ten or twelve hours' start by this time!"

Hardesty whirled and started for the corrals on the run. "Get up your broncs!" he called to the punchers breaking horses in the horse-corral. "We're hittin' the rustler trail!"

CHAPTER ELEVEN

A few minutes saw them ready to ride. Hardesty barked: "Pony, make for Gabe Kyle's Circle K; tell him what's goin' on. He'll bring some of his men. Rusty, you ride to Mart Pincher's!" Tyler he sent to carry word to a couple of other ranchers. They got away at once.

"What the hell, Sale!" Lone protested. "This gettin' word to them gents'll slow us up plenty!"

Hardesty admitted as much. "But this concerns them all," he pointed out coolly. "We've joined forces for the purpose of puttin' an end to such things! . . . We'll wait."

Less than an hour saw Kyle and his foreman arriving. Pony was with them. Rusty and Mart Pincher came soon afterward. Pincher had brought two of his men. When Tyler returned with several more, they were ready to set out.

Lone led the way to the point on the White at which he had spotted the sign of the rustled stuff. The others had their look, grim of face. There was no doubt in the matter. A sizeable bunch of stuff had been hazed off the 6 Lightning and was being driven north.

New as Hardesty might be to cattle raising, he

was an old hand at reading tracks. A glance at these told him all that he needed to know.

"We'll have to fog it!" he clipped off. "Those gents have got nearly twelve hours' start on us—"

They struck out at a ground-covering pace. The trail they followed presented no difficulties. Little effort had been made to conceal it. Whoever had done the rustling had felt reasonably secure from immediate pursuit.

Gabe Kyle broke a silence of several hours' duration to grunt: "Makin' for the Black Hills, looks like."

Hardesty nodded. The sign had not deviated materially from its direct northern trend since they picked it up. The gold camps lay in this direction.

Noon came and passed, and there was little evidence of their having drawn up on the stolen stock. Still they thrust on. It failed to cross their minds that any course lay open save to follow this trail to its end. Somewhere they would come up with the 6 Lightning steers—and if luck was with them, the rustlers as well.

Late in the afternoon the dark bulge of the Black Hills began to loom up on the horizon. They bore a gloomy aspect, those hills; something about them carried a warning. It made no difference to these men.

Sunset found them drawing near the base of the outlying ridges. They pushed on till dusk blotted out the trail. Hardesty drew up and sat peering into the thickening darkness.

"Whoever is pushin' that stuff knew where they were goin'," he murmured to Lone. "They're makin' a beeline—"

Benton assented. "An' not wastin' any time about it," he seconded. "If all I've heard is right, Deadwood must be on ahead somewhere."

"Not much chance of locatin' yore stuff if it reaches there," Mart Pincher broke in gloomily. He was a big man, with a long, lugubrious face. "If we bed down hyar an' wait fer daylight, it shore will, too!"

Hardesty had been considering the matter. Finally he said: "We'll shove on to Deadwood. If the steers aren't there, they can't be far away. It's our best bet."

The others agreed. Delaying only long enough to give the broncs a breathing-spell, they drove on into the night.

Dawn was taking the place of a wan moon, edging the high shoulders of the hills to the west, tumbled and wild and somber, when the cowmen came within striking distance of Deadwood. They crossed the well-beaten stage and freight trail running east, and as daylight strengthened, topped a long rise from which a view of the gold camp could be had.

It lay in a deep valley between bold bluffs: a sprawling tent and cabin and raw-pine city extending from the huddle of saloons fringing the flat at the valley's mouth to the isolated cabins standing among pines a mile away along the town's single street.

Even at this early hour, the place was acrawl with activity. Freight wagons churned up the thick dust; saddle horses and rigs moved through the ruck. But Hardesty took no more than cursory note of these things. His eye roved here and there as he sought some sign of the steers they were tracing.

Pony Johnson exclaimed: "There's a mess uh corrals at the lower end of town, Hard!"

Hardesty nodded. He had already spotted them. "We'll go down and take a look," he said.

They did so. Before they had fairly completed their inspection, Gabe Kyle burst out harshly: "There's yore steers!"

It was true. The 6 Lightning beef, trail-worn and dusty, had been driven into a corral on the grassy flat. A man or two was there. As the cowmen pushed close, looking the stuff over, they grabbed up rifles and one of them moved out threateningly.

"What's wanted, hyar?" he demanded gruffly. Hardesty looked him over carefully.

"Do you lay claim to these steers?"

"What if I do?" was the truculent answer. "It don't make no diff to you!"

Kyle, Pincher and their punchers moved close

menacingly. They were ready for action, and only awaited Hardesty's signal. He warned them with uplifted hand and said to the guard:

"Those steers are mine; they were rustled a couple of nights ago, and I'm takin' 'em away."

It was a flat challenge. For a moment, the silence was thick. Anything could happen here. The guard said flatly:

"Sorry, stranger. That beef was bought las' night by Nick Corson, the butcher . . . Reckon yo're too late—"

"Not much, we ain't!" Lone Benton broke in fiercely. The man stared at him.

"Why ain't yuh?"

"There's the steers, ain't they?" Lone snapped. "An' hyar we are."

"So what?"

"Wal," was the deliberate answer, "I expect yuh won't stop us from takin' 'em away!"

Little as he liked the prospect of violence, Hardesty would not have stopped at that had it been necessary. But at that moment a man came hurrying forward with an air of authority. He was a lank, swarthy individual wearing two bolstered guns and with a shiny law badge pinned on his waist. It was Eph Lawlor, the Deadwood marshal. Someone had gone for him.

"What seems to be the trouble hyar?" he demanded.

Hardesty told him. "I've trailed my rustled

157

steers here, and these gents—" he indicated the cowmen—"came with me to help. This man here," pointing to the guard, "says we can't have the stuff."

Shrewd and dogmatic, Lawlor went into the matter methodically. He had many questions to ask, which Hardesty answered despite the impatience of his companions. At length Lawlor seemed satisfied.

"I reckon yore claim is good, Hardesty," he said at last, reluctantly. "Yuh kin take yore steers—"

"Mighty kind of yuh," Lone told him satirically. "We'd have taken 'em anyways. But what we want is the hombres who sold 'em to this butcher!"

Lawlor could not help him there.

"Corson says he dunno who they was. They rode away las' night soon's the deal was closed." At the muttering which arose, he raised his voice: "What yuh kickin' about? Corson stands to lose more'n you gents on this deal! He paid fer the stuff—"

"That's his lookout," Hardesty came back smoothly. "I still think it's your duty to help us locate the rustlers, marshal!"

Lawlor, however, was not impressed. "I got troubles uh my own. The name on this bill uh sale Corson's got is nothin' but a scrawl; Nick says he never laid eyes on the gents before. Better consider yoreselves lucky, an' forget it!"

The cowmen were already beginning to turn away. "Come on, Hardesty," Mart Pincher urged. "Hell with him! He won't do nothin' for yuh—"

Hardesty was forced to agree. While the guards fell back, muttering, the punchers let down the corral bars and drove the steers out. They were headed back toward their home range.

The return south took longer than the ride to the gold camp had taken, despite the fact that Hardesty turned the steers over to Red Tyler and Rusty Gallup, while he and Lone pushed on ahead with the others. Midmorning of the second day found them within a few miles of the 6 Lightning.

Hardesty pulled up at the point where the other ranchers would branch off toward their own spreads. He, Kyle and Pincher had discussed the matter of the rustling at length without getting anywhere. Kyle said:

"We better call the boys together fer a meetin' before round-up starts. Somethin's got to be done about this!"

Hardesty agreed with him. "Suppose you have your men carry word over west, and I'll do the same for the ranches over this way. We'll meet in MacKinney two days from now and decide what to do. Make sure Pawnee Failes is there." Failes had not been reached in time to come with them this time.

Kyle assented. A few minutes later he and the others jogged away.

The meeting took place on Friday as scheduled. It was held as before, at Henderson's, in MacKinney, and was a warm session, the upshot of which was the decision to go to the commanding officer at Fort Robinson, in view of the absence of any other form of law in the country, and apply for aid in handling the rustlers who threatened to overrun the range. Hardesty and Gabe Kyle were chosen to carry the petition.

They rode there the following day. Captain Hanchard received them affably and listened to what they had to say.

"Of course it's only my opinion," he remarked when they were done; "but you gents were mighty wrathy when Washington instructed me to move you out a while ago. Can't you hit on some means of solving your own problem?"

Hardesty comprehended his drift. Hanchard was suggesting a rope's end for the renegades; a time-honored method of dealing with lawlessness throughout the west. But the trouble was in apprehending the rustlers. So far, though there had been a brush or two at night, not a single one of the guilty men had been identified.

The officer thought it over. "The only thing I can suggest," he said, "is that you petition the U. S. marshal at Sidney for a deputy to clean up this country. Have you done that?"

"No. Much obliged, Hanchard. We'll do that."

Hardesty and Kyle left a moment later. Gabe said:

"Hanchard's proposal is a good one. He ain't authorized to dispense civil justice, himself. But if we kin git a deputy U. S. marshal out yere, our troubles ought to be ironed out in short order."

"If we get a good one," Hardesty agreed.

It was decided, since they would all be driving out to Sidney with their beef-cuts after the round-up, that that would be the time to get word to the federal marshal there.

The round-up had already commenced. New as the scene was for this country, so recently the stamping-ground of Indians, it was an old story for most of the men engaged in it. For Hardesty's part, he was on the cutting-ground day and night when the branding began; yet, he found time to ride to MacKinney one day to visit Glenna MacKinney.

The visit was by no means purposeless, and for that reason Hardesty was somewhat provoked, on arriving at the trading post, to find Lieutenant Dodd there ahead of him. The young officer was obviously interested in the girl, and that she was not entirely indifferent to him was plain from her smiling glances.

She greeted Hardesty pleasantly enough, however. Though she had heard the outcome of the ride to Deadwood, she asked for his version of the affair. Lieutenant Dodd, brushing back his blond hair with a careless hand, listened attentively. At the end he shook his head.

"Too bad you didn't overtake those rustlers, Hardesty," he commiserated.

Hardesty nodded, vaguely irritated even by this display of interest. "It's no more than was to be expected, I suppose."

"But you'll be ready to make your first stock drive to the railroad soon, won't you?" Glenna asked.

He assented. "In two or three days now. That's what I wanted to see you about." He was exasperated at the necessity to speak before Dodd, but thrust on: "You'll be going out to buy your winter supplies soon. Why not make the trip to Sidney with the drive?"

"Why—" He thought Glenna hesitated. "That will be fine, Salem. Yes, I'll go with you."

It rasped him, his errand here satisfactorily completed, to pull away and leave Lieutenant Dodd with her. But he was needed at the round-up; there was really no excuse for delay. Promising to return for her before the drive started, he took his leave.

He was back on the morning of the third day, to find Glenna ready and waiting. She had two wagons which were to be driven out for the supplies she meant to purchase, but she herself rode a lively chestnut mare.

Hardesty never failed to find pleasure in the way she sat her saddle. Often they rode side by side out of the dust beside the trail. There were many things to talk about. Glenna was genuinely pleased with Hardesty's success at ranching; and he had to admit to some complacency on that subject himself, allowing his eye to run over the sizeable herd of two- and three-year-olds which the punchers hazed along in the direction of the railroad and a distant market.

"I started the 6 Lightning at just the right time," he declared. "Five years ago the Sioux would have wiped us out, but now they are becoming so scarce that we have less to worry about from them than from the rustlers."

"Annie Breen finds it a satisfactory business too, if what she tells me is true," Glenna agreed. "I am glad she'll have something to depend on as she grows older."

Hardesty nodded. "There's a sizeable bunch of Annie's Tomahawk steers in with my stuff," he said. "I offered to drive them out and sell them for her, and she accepted."

The drive to Sidney took several days. It could have been even longer without displeasing Hardesty, for he found in the girl an exciting companion.

Sidney was reached one afternoon late. The view of the railroad town across the broad flats was a stirring one; it had grown considerably in a month or two. Piles of railroad supplies stood about its edges; they saw the smoke of busy locomotives, steaming up and down the track; railroad gangs were at work.

"It means prosperity for this country—the Union Pacific," Hardesty declared. "Nothing else could tame the plains quite so quickly."

Sidney itself was a roaring frontier town. The main street was alive with activity. Leaving Lone to get the steers to the railroad shipping pens, newly constructed a mile or so east of town, Hardesty accompanied Glenna to the Platte House, where she meant to stay. She was soon ready for a look at the town.

"Perhaps you'd like to step down to the court house with me," Hardesty proposed. He had told her about his intention to ask the U. S. marshal for a deputy.

Glenna acquiesced. The court house soon came in sight. They were about to step in at the door when a man came toward them along the hall, at sight of whom Hardesty froze with a grunt.

It was Rafe Perrine. But his identity was not the thing which held Hardesty's alert attention, so much as the fact that on Perrine's vest was pinned a deputy U. S. marshal's badge.

If Perrine was surprised by their appearance, he failed to show it, stepping forward with a smile. "Howdy, Glenna," he greeted, sweeping off his hat. His nod to Hardesty was curt.

"How long have you been a deputy marshal?" the latter demanded.

Perrine met his look inscrutably. "Two or three days," was his smooth response. "I've been assigned to western Nebraska, Hardesty—that's your country," he added pointedly. "The district has long stood in need of a thorough clean-up."

Hardesty's jaws ridged. "So that's your game," he rasped slowly. Rafe appeared surprised.

"What do yuh mean?" he demanded.

"You know what I mean!" Hardesty flashed. "You think you're comin' back to MacKinney and have your own way regardless. But don't try any tricks, Perrine! That badge don't mean a thing to me!"

As for Glenna, from the moment of Perrine's appearance she had gone cold and quiet. Convinced as she was that this man was directly responsible for her father's murder, she saw in a twinkling how neatly he had placed himself beyond reach in applying for and procuring an appointment as deputy U. S. marshal. It meant that his grip on the upper Niobrara country would be tighter than ever.

"Why did you have Father killed?" she hurled at him suddenly, her courageous eyes steady.

Perrine opened his wide. Then he chuckled. "Why, that's ridiculous," he scoffed lightly. "You were right there, Glenna. You know I had nothin' whatever to do with it—"

Hardesty shook his head. "It won't go, Perrine. When you made your plans you overlooked one thing—Crow Feather." Tersely he explained what had been learned from the Indian, making it plain that the latter's confession was conclusive.

Perrine shrugged. "Nonsense," he repeated coolly. "Who'd take the word of an Indian?"

Wrath choked Hardesty momentarily. But for the badge on Perrine's vest, he would have called the other to account on the spot. As it was, he could only swallow his chagrin. Perrine seemed to follow his line of thought.

"Besides," he continued easily, a dangerous calm in his tone, "why should I be interested in havin' Glenna's father killed?"

The girl went white. She saw now the position Perrine had her in. If a word was said, Rafe could still drag MacKinney's memory in the dirt. It closed her lips effectually.

Perrine smiled at the glint of fear which showed briefly in her eyes and then vanished; he would have gone on to say more, but Hardesty abruptly turned the girl.

"Come on," he said grimly; "that'll be enough of this." And to Perrine, over his shoulder, as he and Glenna started away: "Go your gait, Perrine; but remember that I've got no reason to hold off from dealin' with you as you deserve! If you know what's good for you, you'll walk wide and talk small!"

166

No more was said, but from the cynical smile that twisted Perrine's lips as he turned casually away, Hardesty made no doubt that his warning had gone for nought.

CHAPTER TWELVE

Winter swooped down that year with a fierceness customary to the northern plains. It did not prevent the steadily increasing volume of traffic from passing through MacKinney during the occasional seasons of calm weather.

Several other buildings had gone up during the fall; the place was beginning to be called a town. Rafe Perrine chose it as his headquarters. On his arrival early in November, he had a rough-board structure run up which he used as an office. It soon became his custom to spend most of the bad weather between Henderson's hotel and the trading post.

It made Glenna furious to have him in her sight, but there was little that she could do about it. He was smoothly, satirically polite to her; nor did her frank display of the loathing she had for him feaze him in the slightest.

She had to admit that he bade fair to be an efficient law enforcement officer, on the surface at least. A drunken cowboy who went on a wild shooting spree shortly before Christmas, in Henderson's place, Perrine mastered easily and promptly. When a case of horse stealing came up a few days later, Perrine took the trail at once and returned within six hours, bringing both the horses and the guilty man. But none of this weighed with the girl. She guessed only too accurately that Perrine must be playing some shrewd game of his own.

For his part, Hardesty agreed with her entirely. He made no doubt that Perrine would soon show his hand in the manner in which he used his power. Nor did it escape Hardesty that the other was in a position to strike at him. That either he or the girl was Rafe's target he felt certain; and he wondered from what direction the first blow would come, and which it would be aimed at.

Meanwhile Perrine suavely busied himself with the concerns of his office. Despite the good intentions of Henderson, and the proprietors of two other saloons which had been built, there was the usual inevitable rough play by miners and cow punchers. Perrine soon gave them to understand that he would tolerate no undue breaking of the peace.

Nor did he spend all his time in MacKinney by any means. More than one rancher gave him to understand that they would depend on him for support in the matter of the rustling, which had not materially slacked off despite Hardesty's prompt action concerning the rustled steers which had been driven to Deadwood.

Perrine promised them he would stop as much of the rustling as it lay in his power to do. He was as good as his word. Every raid that was reported to him he investigated thoroughly; he likewise made occasional counter-moves. Several times he was able to break up raids. Once, with swiftly gathered help, he overhauled a bunch of stolen stock a few miles from their home range; and though the renegades managed to slip away, it was not without a warm exchange of lead.

While no more was definitely learned concerning the identity of the guilty men, Perrine succeeded in making it so hot for them that the loss of steers from rustling fell to almost negligible proportions.

"Somethin' phony about this," was Lone Benton's comment to Hardesty, on learning the facts. "Perrine must be doin' this to warn the rustlers he wants his cut; there ain't no other readin' of his actions . . . Wait'll next spring," he predicted. "The rustlin'll start up ag'in, full blast; an' fer some strange reason, Perrine'll find himself unable to do anythin' about it. You see if I ain't right!"

Hardesty was inclined to agree with him. In the meantime, he had to admit that the effect of Perrine's work was wholly salutary. It puzzled him; for whatever treatment he had told himself he could expect from the man, it was not this.

With a less extensive knowledge of Perrine's past history, the rest of the range was inclined to favor him as a result of his accomplishments.

Hardesty heard many expressions of approbation toward the deputy marshal, in MacKinney and at the stockmen's meetings. He was too shrewd to say anything himself. On the few occasions when they met, Perrine gave him a twisted, inscrutable smile which might mean anything.

"Damn him," Hardesty muttered to himself as he felt the tension of the situation steadily growing. "He's got somethin' up his sleeve; and he's about ready to shake it out . . . The question is, what?"

One day in December, Ep Granger rode into the 6 Lightning yard and demanded to see Hardesty. Granger was a rancher who ran a little spread on Dead Creek, next to the range Pawnee Failes had selected after his fruitless attempt to crowd out Hardesty. Today, Granger was wrathy.

"It's Failes again!" he burst out when Hardesty asked what the trouble was. "My range is better'n his, an' Pawnee's been crowdin' me all along! Tryin' to discourage me, I reckon, drive me out. Wal, this time he's went too fur—"

"What happened, Granger?"

"I found a shot steer over 'long the creek," the quick-tempered rancher blurted. "Nobody saw it done, but I know as well's if his name was printed on the steer that Failes either did it hisself, or had it done! . . . I'm goin' to town for Rafe Perrine, an' by Godfrey, he better do somethin' in a hurry! Will yuh ride in with me, Hardesty?"

The latter agreed. They set out a few minutes later, bundled up against the raw, keening wind. Reaching town in the afternoon, they were so cold that the first thing they thought of was a drink to warm themselves. Taking care of their broncs, they headed for Henderson's place.

As chance would have it, the first person their glances lit on as they stepped in the door was Pawnee Failes. The big fellow was at the bar, yarning companionably with a friend.

Granger forgot all about his drink. He let out a bellow and started for Pawnee. So bitter was his rage that he would have torn the latter apart with his hands in that moment could he have got at him. Hardesty managed to hold him back.

Setting down his drink, Pawnee turned to survey them with well-simulated surprise. "What's bitin' yuh?" he demanded of Granger, at the flood of curses the latter directed at him.

"You know what's botherin' me, yuh damn sneakin' range hog!" was the swift response. "Don't think yuh kin shoot my steers an' git away with it by turnin' up hyar!"

Pawnee scowled blackly. "I never beefed no steer!" he growled the denial, flatly. "When I git ready fer action, Granger, I'll come straight at yuh!"

His use of the singular, however, after what Granger had said, convinced Hardesty that he knew all about the steer-shooting. The rancher

172

saw it too. He would have launched into violent recriminations, but Hardesty stopped him.

"Let Perrine handle this, Ep," he warned. "He's right here in town."

Granger turned away readily, only to halt. "An' jest see to it that yo're right hyar where yuh kin be found, when we come back!" he flung at Pawnee venomously. "It won't be long!"

"I'll be here," the big fellow retorted with so much assurance that Hardesty wondered what he meant. Failes had been a friend and partner of Perrine in the old days. Was this to be the showdown?

Perrine they found in his office. His bushy brows twitched at sight of Hardesty, but he listened to Granger's story with close attention. At its end he put a number of questions. Hardesty was quick to note that he probed the matter as shrewdly as any man could have done. Granger's answers seemed to satisfy him.

"You say Failes is across the street in Henderson's?" he queried, getting to his feet. And at Granger's vehement assent: "We'll just step over and talk to Pawnee."

The latter was still at the bar in Henderson's when they entered. He straightened up, turning; nodded to Perrine. Rafe said:

"Pawnee, Granger here accuses yuh of beefin' one of his steers. What do yuh know about it?"

Failes promptly denied any knowledge of

the matter. But Perrine was not done with him.

"Granger says his range is better than yores. I know that to be a fact. He says yuh been after it, an' knowin' yuh as well as I do, I wouldn't doubt that either." There was nothing but blunt frankness here. "Is this steer-shootin' yore way of goin' about gettin' it, Pawnee?"

Pawnee lost his temper, cursing. "Kin I help it if some low-down coyote takes a shot at his steers?" he flared. "He didn't see me or any of my boys do it—"

"You'd be careful to see to that, wouldn't yuh?" Perrine retorted thinly. He shook his head. "Maybe yuh had nothin' to do with it. I don't know. Anyway, it's just too bad for yuh that it happened in sight of yore range that way . . . Yuh better pay Granger the price of his steer, Pawnee."

Failes's eyes blazed up. Indignation ran away with him. At first he refused flatly to do as Perrine directed. To Hardesty's surprise, Rafe stuck to his point, however.

"I ain't accusin' yuh myself," he pointed out. "All the same, it's up to yuh to see that this sort of thing don't happen so close to yore range, Pawnee. That's a final word."

Pawnee stalled and blustered, shooting darkly accusing looks at Perrine. But in the end he found no alternative but to hand over to Granger the price of his steer. Ep took it with an ill grace.

"Yuh ain't foolin' nobody, declarin' yuh never done it!" he told Pawnee grimly. "By rights, I ought to take it out of yore hide with a gun. If it happens ag'in, I will!"

Perrine put an end to this bickering. At his suggestion, Hardesty and Granger soon rode out of town on the way to their ranches. They were scarcely out of sight before Pawnee swung out of Henderson's and headed for the deputy marshal's office. He found Perrine alone.

"What was the idea of that play, Rafe?" he began raspingly. "What if I did plug one of Granger's steers? Is this yore way of servin' notice that yo're throwin' yore old friends down cold?"

Perrine eyed him coolly, and a thin smile touched his lips.

"Forget it, Pawnee. What's the price of a single steer to yuh? That was a fool trick anyway, knockin' a steer over close to the creek like that. It didn't fool even Granger for a second!"

Pawnee would have argued the matter heatedly, but Perrine waved him to silence.

"Wait," he said. "Don't go off the handle. Our day is comin'—"

Pawnee regarded him suspiciously. "What yuh mean, our day?" he demanded. "I don't get yuh."

"You will," was the answer. "The time is comin' when I'll be the boss of this country. Then there'll be some real pickings."

"Boss of it now, pret' near, ain't yuh?"

Perrine's hard smile broadened. "That's a matter of opinion," he returned. "I mean to clinch it . . . There's talk already of Nebraska becoming a state. A government will be formed. There'll be chances for a man to grow mighty big. That's my aim." He paused. "Runnin' guns taught me the folly of botherin' about small change. It's my slant exactly on rustlin' . . . Wait," he counseled afresh. "Our day is comin', faster than yuh think. You'll be glad then that yuh held off."

Pawnee was forced to be content with that.

The story of Perrine's part in the matter of the beefed steer spread rapidly. It made a good impression. Men remembered that Perrine and Pawnee Failes had once been associates. Rafe's promptness in bringing his friend to book satisfied men of the seriousness with which he regarded his work.

If the range in general was impressed by the Solomon-like quality of Perrine's law giving, however, Hardesty and Glenna MacKinney were not. It seemed to warn them that the man's nefarious designs were even deeper than they supposed.

Hardesty had occasion to think much over the matter, for he rode to MacKinney often as the bleak, gray days of December lengthened in number. More than once he found that, as before, Lieutenant Dodd had forestalled him by riding over from Fort Robinson to see Glenna. The girl seemed to enjoy his company.

For the most part, however, Hardesty was too busy with the broadening concerns of a successful rancher to give much attention to his rival. Dodd was a novelty to the girl, he told himself; brass buttons always appealed superficially to women. Glenna would get over that shortly and reach a more accurate estimate of the man underneath. Dodd was all right, of course, but he was young, of the flashy, adventurous type. Glenna was not for him.

But if Hardesty was able to put the matter away from him, Lone Benton and Dublin Annie Breen took it more seriously. Annie rode to MacKinney more often than ever, these days; she saw what was going on. Lone knew too. He found in it an excuse for riding to Annie's place for a talk with her.

"I dunno what Sale kin be thinkin' of, lettin' matters drift like this," he expressed himself gloomily. "Him an' that girl are jest made fer each other. He's gone on 'er, too. But he'll never git 'er this way!"

Annie sagely agreed. "Somethin'," she said practically, "will have to be done, an' done soon. I'll see what I can hit on."

But if Hardesty and his friends were busy with their own concerns, so was Perrine. He knew he was gaining ground rapidly on this range, yet he cast about for some means of settling the matter once and for all.

It was not long before his agile brain supplied a solution. On the same day, a messenger in the form of one of Pawnee Failes's punchers pulled out for the Black Hills. He was gone three days, and on his return there rode with him a second man, who drew up a couple of miles outside of MacKinney as the short, overcast afternoon drifted toward its close, while the messenger continued on his way. Later in the evening, however, the second man rode on toward town through the enfolding gloom. Circling the short street, he drew up behind Rafe Perrine's office, dismounted, and stole forward.

There was a light in Perrine's place, though the new jail was dark. The newcomer made sure Rafe was there alone, then made for the door and knocked.

Perrine admitted him. A nod of recognition passed between them; there was in the visitor's eyes a look of inquiry. He was Abe Slater, the man whose wild shot at the Indian had killed Colin MacKinney, at the trading post.

"Curly located yuh, eh?" said Perrine. Slater's nod was curt.

"What yuh want of me, Rafe?" There was a touch of uncertainty in the question. Perrine ignored it for the moment, asking how Abe had

178

been getting along. Slater had been in hiding in the Black Hills. He brushed all this aside impatiently.

"Give me the story," he urged.

Perrine sat thoughtful for a moment, and when he spoke it was to approach his subject obliquely. "How'd you like to be able to go anywhere yuh want to again, Abe?"

"Can't I now?" Slater countered. Rafe waved a disposing hand.

"I'd be forced to toss you in the jug for killin' MacKinney in a minute, here in town. You know it."

The hunted look in Abe's glance said that he did. "What kin we do?" he asked.

Perrine leaned forward. "Get the jump on 'em," he said. "Give yoreself up. Let me put yuh in a cell. You'll come up for trial in a couple weeks; the circuit judge'll be on hand then. You'll get off easy. I know; I'll see to it that yuh do. I can promise that. Then you'll be in the clear . . . Well?"

Apprehension tightened Slater up at the mere suggestion. At first he was dead against the proposal. It took a lot of talk to make him see matters Perrine's way, but at length Rafe succeeded.

"Yo're shore there won't be no hitch?" Abe demanded for the fourth or fifth time.

"No," Perrine allayed his fears by speaking

positively. "How can there? . . . Leave it all to me. I'll take care of things."

Abe stood up. "Okay. I reckon yuh can lock me up."

There was no one else in the jail at the time. Perrine put him in a cell, supplied him with food, and left him. In the morning, Rafe got up his horse and rode away from MacKinney. Several men saw him go; Lone Benton among them. He did not return until after dark, nor did anyone watch his return, for he made sure of that.

The following morning, Glenna was astonished to learn that Perrine had "picked up" her father's slayer, brought him to town and put him in the lockup. There could be no doubt, for Henderson told her of having gone to the jail, where he saw Abe Slater lodged in a cell. The news spread rapidly. While the death of MacKinney meant little to these men who had arrived in the country after it happened, the prospect of a shooting trial interested them. All day the topic was aired in the saloons. Those who claimed to know declared Slater's neck was as good as in a noose already.

Hardesty heard the news that night. He could not understand Perrine's object, and was inclined to disbelieve. Accordingly, he planned to ride to MacKinney the following morning for a talk with Glenna on the subject.

But even while Hardesty was laying his plans, Perrine had begun to play out his hand as it suited him. With early dark, after first making sure that no one was about, he lit a lantern and passed back into the jail. Slater met him with a snarl of irritation from his cell.

"Whyn't yuh do somethin' about a fire in here?" he complained. "It's cold as hell, Rafe!" Nor was he exaggerating. His teeth were chattering, and he shivered.

Ignoring the appeal, Perrine opened the cell and stepped inside. His face was grave. Watching him, Abe jerked out suddenly: "What's bitin' yuh, anyway?"

"I've got bad news for yuh, Abe—"

"How's that?" Slater tightened with suspicion. Perrine shook his head soberly.

"Lots of talk about yore case. They're figurin' to put yuh away. I'm afraid—"

"Yuh gotta let me outa this, then!" Abe exclaimed. "Yuh said yuh could work it shore—!"

"I know. But—" And Perrine hesitated again.

Abe was like a hunted animal in a flash. "I'm gettin' outa here!" he rasped. "Gimme my gun, Rafe, an' lemme go!"

Perrine shook a regretful negative. "I can't do that."

Abe reached his feet in a bound. The cell-door was open; he was painfully conscious of the fact. Words came out of him in a rush: "Yuh dirty, double-crossin'—"

"None of that!" Perrine grated. "Yuh gave yoreself up, Abe! Now yo're stayin'!" He might have been playing with Slater like a cat with a mouse, so final was his ultimatum; but all this escaped Abe.

Suddenly he sprang at Perrine. With a wrench he strove to possess himself of one of Perrine's guns. Rafe flung him off. Slater sprang for the door, cursing madly.

Perrine's gun crashed as Abe reached the office door. He never got through. Staggering with a muffled cry, he crumpled there in the door and lay still. He was dead.

Except for dragging him into another cell and straightening him out on the cot, Perrine paid him little further attention. Thoughtfully, he smashed the lantern, tore his own clothes in a place or two, and gave the jail the general appearance of a savage struggle. It was not difficult.

Then Rafe went into the office to wait for the men whose booted feet he already heard approaching on the run.

When Hardesty arrived in town the following morning, it was to learn that Abe Slater, MacKinney's slayer, had made a desperate attempt to escape jail and that Perrine had been forced to kill him. The story was circumstantial in the extreme; Henderson and others vouched for its truth. Hadn't they seen the jail afterward?

Slater had succeeded in getting out of his cell, and Perrine had had to shoot him at the office door. There was a bloodstain there, where he had fallen.

Hardesty went directly to Glenna. The trading post, or store as it was now called, was busy, but she found a few minutes to talk to him.

"It's bewildering," she confessed frankly. "Perrine's action makes me wonder if he has not acted in good faith throughout. Why should he have brought his former companion to justice, unless he meant to solve Father's shooting?"

She was obviously impressed. Remembering that all the men he had talked to were likewise impressed, and in Perrine's favor, Hardesty believed he found in the fact an answer for what must otherwise remain a dark enigma. Clear to be seen, how completely Perrine had in this one master stroke cleared himself of all complicity, of any slightest breath of suspicion even, in the matter of Colin MacKinney's coldly calculated murder!

Hardesty told himself that he wasn't fooled for a minute. Glenna too, would regain her balance after a time; see the mistake she had made in underestimating Perrine's devious cunning. In the meantime, Hardesty was left practically alone to wait for his enemy's first act of open hostility, and to wonder as never before what form it would take.

CHAPTER THIRTEEN

Stanch and sturdy in the saddle, muffled to the ears, Annie Breen rode toward MacKinney over the light snow which had fallen the night before. It was three days before Christmas. Annie was in no hurry, for she was going to see Glenna today, and not yet had she hit on the plan she had promised Lone to devise for throwing Hardesty and the girl together.

The coming festivities appeared an ideal occasion for her stratagem, but just what it was to be escaped her.

She was within a few miles of town when a cheerful hail dragged her out of her abstraction. She turned to see Lieutenant Dodd approaching by the cut-off trail to Fort Robinson. She and young Dodd had never enjoyed more than a speaking acquaintance, but this morning she greeted him warmly.

He too, was heading for town. She knew what his errand was there.

"We'll have a white Christmas, Left'nant," she smiled.

He nodded, pulling the collar of his overcoat higher around his ears against the raw bite of the keening wind. "We always do. More snow will fall, if the weather moderates a bit."

"Not enough to spoil the season's doin's, though," Annie rejoined purposefully. Inspiration had come to her in a flash on seeing the young officer. She had no trouble steering the talk in the right direction. "I suppose ye'll be enjoyin' yerself, Christmas Eve?"

"We're having an affair at the post," he assented. She gazed at him with affected surprise.

"You mean ye won't be in town with Glenna, then?" she demanded with the impulsiveness of a question which came out before she could guard her tongue. Dodd appeared slightly uncomfortable at this frankness.

"I might be, if I'm asked," he muttered. The question of just where he would be on the big night had actually been bothering him more than he cared to admit.

Annie rode for a while in silence. Finally she said: "Well, I don't hold much with soldier doin's. But I suppose ye *could* have wimmen at the post? Why don't ye ask Glenna to come?"

Guileless despite her persistence, Dodd was really surprised by this simple proposal. It had never occurred to him. A flush suffused his lean, strongly cut cheeks. "Do you really think she would come?" He attempted to hide his eagerness under a casual tone, but Annie caught it.

"Come?" She snorted. "Why shouldn't she come? It'll save her the work of makin' a party at her place," she pointed out with homespun practicality. The irony of it escaped Dodd.

"Captain Hanchard would be delighted, I know," he drove on hopefully. "It would be great fun. We're decorating the mess hall—and there could be a dance!" He went on to confide other details. Dublin Annie listened indulgently.

"Then why don't ye ask Glenna straight off, gilly?" she demanded brusquely. "A goose could see the store you men set by such fun."

He flashed her a chivalrous grin. "Then I will ask her—if you'll accept an invitation also, ma'am!"

Annie knew by that how grateful he was for her insistence. She laughed. "O' course I'll come," she agreed with her usual brusqueness. "Think ye could keep me away?"

It was so settled. In the back of her wily mind, Annie was congratulating herself: "This'll give Sale Hardesty somethin' to think about, I reckon! When he sees how things are goin', he'll speak up before it's too late."

They reached town shortly afterward, and found Glenna at the store. Business being slack, she invited them into her sitting-room. There was considerable amusement for Annie in the means by which Lieutenant Dodd finally arrived at his invitation to the girl. His very indirection revealed his earnestness.

Glenna, however, was gratifyingly surprised.

She hesitated over her answer. It had never occurred to her that she should have her Christmas Eve party anywhere but here. She had only been waiting for someone from the 6 Lightning to appear before she extended an invitation to the entire outfit. She admitted as much.

"Why not invite everybody to the fort, then?" Annie thrust in. "After all, it's Christmas!"

"I'm sure Captain Hanchard would agree," Dodd seconded.

Glenna was persuaded. "I'll come, if you think it is all right," she told him.

"I'll send word to all the ranches I can reach, the minute I get the Captain's consent," he promised her. "In fact, he has suggested something of the sort in the past."

If Annie was entirely successful this far, however, she had no intention of letting it go at that. She made a point of stopping in at the 6 Lightning on her way home that afternoon. Hardesty was busy as usual, but he dropped what he was doing, insisting that she come in the cabin long enough to warm herself.

"I've come from town," she opened up abruptly, watching him closely.

"That so?" Hardesty's face lit up. He thought he knew what was coming.

"Sale—" She met his eye steadily. "There's goin' to be a Christmas Eve party at Fort Robinson Friday. Glenna's been invited, an' she's goin'."

Hardesty's face fell. He needed no more to tell him how matters stood.

"You'll be gettin' an invite, yerself," Annie proceeded, watching him narrowly. He had control of himself by now. His disappointment showed only in the sobriety of his answer.

"Afraid I won't be able to make it," he said slowly. "I suppose you'll be there, though?"

She ignored that. Her tone flattened: "Don't be a fool about this, Salem Hardesty! Ye must know what's goin' on. Here's this young whippersnapper, Dodd, makin' love to Glenna; an' what's more, he's gittin' somewheres, takin' her clear away like this!" She let that sink in. "Think ye're foolin' me a bit? You want Glenna. Why not do somethin' about it?"

He thought it over, face inscrutable. And then, after a delay: "You're pretty sure I'll be invited to the fort?"

"Ye'll be invited," she assured him.

"Then maybe I'll manage to get there, at that."

"Shure ye will! . . . Ye might even go fer the girl, an' take her," Annie pursued craftily. But Hardesty shook his head.

"Dodd's invited Glenna. She'll expect him to come for her." Nor would he budge from this stand. Annie had to be content with what she had accomplished. She left shortly, satisfied the seed she had planted in his mind would take root and grow.

Lone met her almost accidentally as she was pulling away. "Bound home?" he said diffidently. "I'm headin' north. I'll ride with yuh."

Annie's eyes twinkled. "Mr. Benton," she said primly, "we had words lately about Glenna MacKinney an' that knothead ye work for. I'll have ye know I've arranged everything."

Lone evinced surprise. "Sho'!" he exclaimed, admiringly. "You wimmen! . . . How'd ye manage it, ma'am?"

"Wait," she counseled. "Ye'll soon enough find out fer yerself."

Lone kept at her, but she had lost interest in the subject. With the affairs of others ironed out to her satisfaction, she could give her attention entirely to her own concerns. They consisted chiefly of evading Lone's questions until he was ready to explode with exasperation.

Hardesty received his invitation to attend the Christmas Eve party at Fort Robinson, late the following day. It decided him. While he knew Dublin Annie had a woman's reason for speaking as she did about Glenna and young Dodd, he could not hide from himself the truth of her words. The officer was making a determined play for Glenna's favor. That he was gaining ground could scarcely be better indicated than by the girl's acceptance of his invitation to the post.

It was time for Hardesty to act.

Since his return to Nebraska after getting out of the army, he had fully intended that Glenna should one day become his wife. He had based his every move on that expectation. From the beginning he had felt that Glenna was agreeable. As yet, however, he had not spoken to her about it. Perhaps she had grown tired of waiting.

"I'll speak to her at the party," he resolved. "Annie's right; there's no need of lettin' this go on. I'd never forgive myself if I found I'd waited too long already."

It was in this mood that he headed for Fort Robinson with the others on Friday. The entire outfit had been invited; all had accepted. Hardesty understood that other outfits were to attend as well. There was even to be music—fiddling, at least, an army drum and horn.

Annie Breen, and the two men she had working for her now to handle her stock, had gone on ahead. But it was not of Dublin Annie that Hardesty was thinking as he neared the military post late in the afternoon. Had Glenna arrived yet? Should he have gone for her after all?

His doubts were allayed by the arrival of a light rig which pulled up as he and the boys were taking care of their broncs. Lieutenant Dodd was driving; Glenna was with him. She was looking prettier than ever today, her eyes sparkling; she waved a laughing greeting to Hardesty; but Dodd was on the ground and handing her out of the rig before Hardesty could reach them.

Entering the post in a group, they were welcomed by Captain Hanchard. He had laid aside his military bearing for the occasion, and was a smiling, affable host.

Dublin Annie was animatedly chaffing several cattlemen who had also arrived early. Two stout, good natured matrons, the wives of ranchers, were being showered with the gallantries of the soldiers. Punchers stood about in knots, grins of anticipation on their weathered, homely faces.

Toward dusk, others who had been invited began to arrive. There were many in the cheerful crowd which filled the little two-company post to overflowing; army freighters, bearded frontiersmen still wearing buckskin and moccasins; a colorful gathering. The log building had been decorated with evergreen boughs; a few clusters of last fall's berries had been found.

Rafe Perrine entered with a flourish, to be greeted heartily. Plainly he had succeeded in making himself popular with the people of this country.

Lone watched him shaking hands with the ranchers, a scowl on his seamed visage. "Ain't he a little tin god?" he grunted to Hardesty.

For his part, Hardesty kept out of the deputy marshal's way. He could not give Perrine his approval, and there was no point in a clash.

Hardesty noted, too, that Glenna managed to avoid Rafe's suave attentions. Whether it meant that she had changed her mind about him again, was not clear, but Lieutenant Dodd claimed so much of her time that she may have found opportunity for nothing else.

The fact that she found no time for him, either, seemed to carry an ominous implication. Busy as he was with the manner in which he should plead his cause with her, he began to wonder whether he would even have the chance he needed.

Supper was announced when it became clear that all had arrived who were coming. Everyone trouped into the mess-hall, noisy with good humor. The hall had likewise been decorated: lamps shone on the happy faces from a dozen brackets along the wall; at one end a huge flag had been draped, garnished with crossed swords.

All this was lost on Hardesty, however. It had suddenly come into his head that this was his chance; that if he could reach Glenna in time, she would eat with him, and he could have his say under cover of the laughter and talk around the table. But he found himself too late; Lieutenant Dodd had forestalled him. Hardesty's first glimpse of Glenna was of her going into the mess-hall on the young officer's arm.

Hardesty fell back to rejoin Lone and the boys. He paid no attention to the jab from her elbow which Dublin Annie gave him as she passed, but his mood was scarcely lightened by the fact that Annie had captured his Texan foreman and was bearing him away in triumph.

The meal, though great pains had been lavished on it by the army cooks, was not a pleasant one for Hardesty. Again and again his eye drifted to Glenna, where she sat with an officer on either side of her. She appeared happier than he had ever seen her. Once she caught his eye. She smiled brightly. Hardesty attempted to respond, but it was hardly a success.

After supper the tables were cleared away and a corner roped off for the musicians. The dance was soon in full swung.

Despite the scarcity of women, the floor was full of whirling couples. Captain Hanchard was first to claim Glenna, guiding her through the deliberate intricacies of a waltz; soldiers were paired off, and swayed with the rest. Even so, many men stood on the sidelines, talking as they watched.

The steady development of this country was the topic which held the attention of most. Hardesty found himself near Rafe Perrine, who was discussing with Gabe Kyle the possibility of Nebraska's becoming a state in the spring.

"There seems to be no question about it," Perrine was saying sagely. "I understand it's a matter of Washington politics. There'll soon be a convention in Omaha, and a little later we'll be forming our county government—"

"By grab, that's a fact!" Kyle exclaimed, and added: "We couldn't find a better man than you to represent us in Omaha, Perrine. Would yuh be willin' to go?"

Hardesty moved away, his lips twisting in a crooked smile. He had no doubt what Perrine's answer to that question would be.

The dance ended a moment later. Hardesty had been watching Glenna. For a moment, she stood unattended. Resolve caught him up and he started for her. Before he could arrive, Lieutenant Dodd appeared at her side. He said something. Glenna nodded smiling assent; Hardesty saw her lift her arms just as the music started for the next dance.

He fell back, his face bleak. It appeared plain enough the girl had no time for him. For ten minutes he watched Glenna gliding in Dodd's arms. The officer was animated; he kept up a steady flow of conversation to which the girl responded readily. Hardesty's jaws ridged. Abruptly he turned and started for the door.

Lone and Dublin Annie whirled by at the moment and caught sight of him. "Where yuh goin', Sale?" the Texan called.

Hardesty barely paused for his answer. "It's gettin' late," he said. "I'll pull out for the ranch. You and the boys can come on when you get ready." The next moment he was through the door and gone.

Something like consternation flashed across Annie Breen's features. She had scarcely been able to believe her ears, for she knew Hardesty had had no opportunity as yet to approach Glenna, let alone talk with her. Annie was so surprised by his departure that for the moment she could find nothing to say. Lone regarded her darkly.

"Is this the way yuh fixed things up fer Sale?" he inquired bitingly. "Because I don't think much of it!"

As for Hardesty, he lost no time in getting into his wraps and pulling his bronc out of the heap. A moment later he struck out alone for home. He was dejected.

"She don't want any part of me," he brooded bitterly. "Annie was right, and I put off speakin' up till it was too late. Dodd's had time to make his play for Glenna, and he's won!"

CHAPTER FOURTEEN

The long winter dragged to its end at last. Hardesty had found it a busy one for him; scarcely a month passed on this high northern range but the stock was menaced in some new manner. If it was not an ice storm, then the snow fell six or eight feet deep on the level, with the drifts twice as heavy in the coulees, and the cattle reduced to browsing on high brush or the tender bark of young trees.

Hardesty found no fault with the necessity to watch his stock incessantly, however. Believing as he did that Glenna was lost to him, he was glad of the work which drove thought of his own troubles from his mind. He even went so far as to double his tasks needlessly, though he told himself it was because there was nothing better to do.

For some reason Lone clung to him closer than was his usual wont. His companionship was a relief in a way. And yet, if there were times when nothing could assuage the essential loneliness which attacked Hardesty, by neither word nor sign did he indicate the cause of it to the Texan.

Lone watched him solicitously and shook his head more than once. He was inclined to blame the whole affair, with its disastrous outcome, on Dublin Annie. "Dang meddlin' wimmen!" was the way he expressed himself, disgustedly. "If they'd keep their nose out, things'd be better all round!"

Curiously enough, the sincerity of his stand did not prevent him from riding often to the little place on Ghost Creek to argue amiably with Annie. They kept up a half-serious feud on the subject of Hardesty; Annie was forced to defend herself vigorously to cover her own sense of chagrin, for there could no longer be any doubt that her Christmas ruse had gone wide of the mark.

"Sale give up too easy!" she gave it as her opinion, stoutly. "Seems like a man'll never learn his cause ain't lost till the last cat's hung—I mean, till the girl's married the other feller, an' it's all over but the squallin'."

"A man's got his pride," Lone declared sagely. "If a gal shows him pretty plain she ain't got no interest in him—"

Annie snorted disdainfully. "You an' yore pride!" she retorted with scorn. "Yore bull-headedness, yuh mean!"

If Hardesty noted Lone's penchant for drifting toward Ghost Creek every time a bad storm struck, to make sure Annie Breen had come through it safely, he made no comment.

Not until spring lay on the land, with the buds

swelling above the sparkling snow water and the blackbirds skimming overhead in joyous song, did he ride to MacKinney again; and then only because the rumor reached him that events were transpiring which interested him in spite of himself.

While he did not see Glenna in town, he returned with the news that Nebraska had newly become a state. There was even strong agitation for the formation of Wyoming Territory.

"Gabe Kyle, Pincher and the others are deep in plans for a local government," Hardesty told his crew at supper. "There's an Omaha Convention sittin' now. They're pickin' a delegate to send off to it."

"Perrine?" Lone grunted. Hardesty's answer was a nod, and for some moments silence held. Not a man in this outfit but had Hardesty's own attitude toward the deputy marshal. None of Perrine's fence-mending since he had pinned on the law badge had succeeded in changing their minds about him.

"Somebody oughta show up that buzzard while there's time!" Lone averred. "Let him go his gait, an' he'll be gittin' big—"

"There's more men watchin' him now than there was when we drove into this country," Hardesty pointed out. "He'll come a cropper if he tries any of his rough stuff. I'm just waitin' for that to happen."

"An' in the meantime, he's free to raise hell any way it suits him!" Lone retorted. He shook his grizzled head ominously. "I told yuh last fall what we could expect from him. I ain't found any reason yet to change my mind."

But if the 6 Lightning was dubious of the rectitude of his intentions, Perrine himself was serenely confident of the steadfastness of his guiding star. There was reason for this, with most of the stockmen on this range behind him. Without a qualm he set off for Omaha in March, full of great plans for the country. He was back within three weeks. Hardesty got the news from Gabe Kyle, meeting the latter one day on the range.

"Perrine is a good man," Kyle declared with conviction. "He was made county commissioner, an' fer one, I'm glad of it—"

"Results are what we want," Hardesty nodded woodenly. "I've got nothin' to say against any man who'll give them to us."

"It means we'll have our own law," Gabe pursued, "without the necessity for dependin' on the federal marshal at Sidney."

Hardesty had foreseen this development; he thought he had seen even further into the future, where that was concerned, than Kyle or his friends.

"Has Perrine appointed a sheriff yet?" he queried.

"Yeh. He's picked Pawnee Failes." Gabe appeared embarrassed at the necessity to admit the fact. "Looks from hyar like that choice wasn't so good, but I expect a man's entitled to at least one mistake. It may even be that Rafe knows Failes better'n we do."

Hardesty reflected grimly that there could be little doubt of this. The appointment of Pawnee to the office of sheriff was the first crack to appear in Perrine's armor; it seemed a certain indication of what might be expected from now on. Failes had never pretended to a troublesome honesty; his standing on this range had never been of the best.

"If Failes has been appointed," Hardesty said, "it won't be long before we know what he intends to do."

Kyle understood him. With the confirmation of spring, and the gradual shrinking of the big drifts in the shady spots, the round-up was just around the corner. Gabe sought Hardesty out one day with the announcement of a stockmen's meeting at which the details of the work were to be decided.

"I suppose Pawnee will be givin' up his Diamond Cross, now that he's sheriff," Hardesty remarked casually. Yet he waited for the answer, believing he knew what it would be.

"No, I understand he's hangin' on to the spread," Gabe responded. Hardesty was not surprised.

"Then I reckon we'll be tallyin' his stuff as usual," he said.

Whatever the deeper thought in his mind, he did not voice it, but it was no more than he expected when, a couple of days later, Lone sought him out with something he had discovered.

"I thought we all agreed not to be brandin' mavericks on the sly," the Texan opened bluntly. It was just his way. He knew well enough what had been decided.

"That's right," Hardesty nodded. "What about it?"

"Pawnee Failes's men are doin' it, that's all," Lone told him flatly. "Pony was the one who got wise to it; he come acrost a fresh-branded calf back in the busted land over south. It was wearin' Pawnee's Diamond Cross. He told me about it, an' I rode over there. Danged if I didn't spot a Diamond Cross waddy with a calf down in a coulee, an' a brandin' fire goin'!"

Hardesty's look was sober.

"Just where was that?" he asked. Lone told him, and he nodded. "Mighty close to Ep Granger's range . . . You didn't happen onto any sore-footed cows without a calf?"

Lone said no. "But what difference does that make? Does Pawnee think, now he's sheriff, that the rules we made fer all of us don't apply to him? By grab, I'll have plenty to say t'morrow night at that stockmen's meetin'!"

"No—" Hardesty spoke slowly, deliberately. "You won't say a word, Lone. I think I see where this is headin'. We'll wait till the round-up and see what happens . . . I want you and the boys to be sure and comb those branded mavericks out of the rough with the gather, though," he added. "Pawnee's men'll shove 'em back in the breaks where they might be missed. Just be sure they aren't."

With a pretty fair idea of what Hardesty intended, Lone assented to the plan.

The ranchers met the following night in MacKinney as planned, and the details of the round-up were ironed out. Pawnee Failes was there, importantly wearing his sheriff's badge. If Hardesty needed assurance that Failes was as crooked as ever, he received it when the subject of mavericks was touched on and Pawnee passed it over without a word. Had he been square and above board, he would have announced on the spot that he was branding mavericks ahead of time.

Lone shot Hardesty a meaning look, but the latter warned him to silence with a flicker of his eyelids. The time for action had not yet come.

The round-up started the following morning. With the withdrawal of constant Indian threats, stock had multiplied on this range speedily. The gather took almost a week, the chuck wagon moving over a wide area, sometimes covering as much as twenty miles in a single day.

On the afternoon that several mavericks, fresh-branded Diamond Cross, were thrown in with the bunch, Hardesty managed to reach camp early. None of the mavericks had been spotted by others, but the branding was to begin tomorrow. Hardesty waited.

Long before dawn, the cavvy was hazed in to camp with a rush of hoofs and thrown into a rope corral; presently the cook gave his morning call. There were half a dozen outfits gathered here, and representatives of as many more. The sun had not yet pushed above the horizon when they fell to the task of cutting the great herd held on a grassy flat a mile from camp.

Within an hour, Ep Granger, one of the cutters, let out a roar on discovering one of the branded mavericks. "What's the meanin' of this?" he bellowed, whirling in his saddle to glare at Pawnee Failes. "Hyar's a calf with yore brand on it—not two weeks old, yuh damned crook!"

Every man within hearing tightened up at this flat challenge. Pawnee pushed forward authoritatively, face dark.

"What's that?" he snapped. "Be careful what yo're sayin', Granger!"

"The hell with yore advice, Failes! Yuh better explain this branded maverick—an' talk fast!"

With the evidence before his eye, Pawnee knew better than to attempt a denial. He tried another tack, staring at the calf in surprise and then pretending indignation.

"I never branded that critter!" he declared. "I dunno nothin' about it . . . Somebody done this to git me in a jam! I got enemies; I know that. But by God, if I find out who they are—"

"Quit lyin'!" Granger blazed at him. "Yuh know all there is to know about this calf, Pawnee; an' there's another one, if there's any mistake about it—" he drove on as a second youngster, motherless and bearing the Diamond Cross iron, was run out of the big herd. "That's my beef, like as not! I always suspected yuh of gittin' into my stuff, but I wasn't shore jest how it was bein' done!"

Cornered fairly, his wrath aflame, Pawnee faced his accuser across ten feet of open space, and for a moment the threat of violence here was strong.

"What yuh mean?" Pawnee rasped harshly.

"You know what I mean!" Ep charged. "Prob'ly the steer yuh beefed was the mother of one of these calves, an' mebby there was others we didn't find! Yuh never intended this fresh-branded stuff to show in the round-up gather—but there was a slip-up somewheres. An' now, by Godfrey, we got yuh dead to rights!"

Hardesty, listening keenly, saw that it would not have required the bad blood between these two to set off the dynamite in this situation.

There would have been gunplay on the spot had not Gabe Kyle and himself thrust in between. Hardesty faced Pawnee and his opening words were grim.

"We all heard, Failes," he said. "What've you got to say for yourself?"

Pawnee attempted to laugh the matter off. "If my boys've been runnin' an iron on the stray stuff they found on the range, I never knowed it," he declared boldly. "I'll have to speak to 'em—"

"You'll do more than speak to 'em!" Hardesty flung back. "You'll give Ep Granger a bill of sale for every branded maverick we find with the gather; and if anything like this happens again, you won't talk yourself out of it! Is that plain?"

Pawnee blustered, scowling his rage. But a darting glance at the ring of faces showed him the others were with Hardesty to a man. Still he remained defiant. His glare fastened on Hardesty.

"Yo're takin' a whole lot on yoreself, Hardesty! Mebby there's somethin' personal in this."

But Hardesty was not to be subdued by his menacing tone. "Maybe there is," he bit off. "You can make just as much of it as you please, Failes; and I mean right now!"

This acceptance of his challenge was a little too quick for Pawnee. "I'll remember this, Hardesty," was the best he could do. "Don't forget who yo're talkin' this way to," he muttered as he turned away.

"I ain't likely to—or what you're sayin', either," was Hardesty's final, biting retort. "Come at me any time, Failes. You'll find me ready and waitin'!"

One of the witnesses of the clash between Pawnee and Hardesty was Dublin Annie Breen, who had decided to be present at least at the branding.

While she approved heartily of Hardesty's stand in the matter of the mavericks, at the same time she recognized a hardness about him which was new. Annie had a broad experience of life. She saw Hardesty turning into a secretly embittered, iron-handed man. Her conscience told her what was the cause of it.

It was all her fault; nor did she try to hide the fact from herself. The question was what she could do to rectify her blunder. With the best intention in the world she had thrown Glenna MacKinney into Lieutenant Dodd's arms. Nothing she could say to Hardesty could make up to him for that.

"It's that girl," she thought vexedly. "She ought to get a good talkin' to! Can't she see what she's doin' to him?"

It needed no more than the suggestion for Annie to act upon it. That afternoon she abandoned the round-up without excuse, and early evening saw her approaching MacKinney, a gleam of purpose in her eyes.

Glenna she found getting supper. "Come in," the girl told her, "you're just in time, Annie. I thought you were at the round-up."

Annie divested herself of her wraps, and promptly rolled up her sleeves. It was never her habit to partake of a meal which she had not helped prepare. Not until they sat down, and the first edge of appetite was dulled, did she open her subject; and even then it was plain she meant to make no confessions she found unnecessary.

"How are ye gettin' on these days?" she demanded abruptly.

"Very well," Glenna smiled, knowing her friend's ways. "Have you any particular reason for wanting to know?"

"I don't see much of Salem Hardesty around any more," Annie proceeded evenly. The girl's smile faded.

"Don't you?" she murmured.

Annie eyed her briefly, and took the plunge. "Do ye like this young Dodd feller a lot, dearie?"

"Why, of course he's very pleasant—" Glenna hesitated. "What do you mean, Annie?"

"I mean it's fer the likes of him that Sale Hardesty stays away," was the blunt response. Glenna colored.

"I'm sorry if he feels that way . . ." She was a little bewildered. Had she given Salem cause for offence, even unknowingly?

Annie saw there was nothing for it but to

make a clean breast of the business. She did the job thoroughly, not attempting to spare herself; Glenna listened with slowly widening eyes, consternation knocking at her heart, as the older woman told how she had persuaded Lieutenant Dodd to invite her to Fort Robinson at Christmas, hoping that a natural feeling of jealousy on Hardesty's part would make him speak his mind. The girl showed less resentment than Annie would have expected of her, proving extremely reluctant to discuss the matter at all.

But Dublin Annie was nothing if not thorough. Far from satisfied with the results of her talk with Glenna, with whom she believed she had squared Hardesty, Annie put herself in the latter's way the following morning as the tail end of the round-up was being cleaned up. Before she could speak, he said:

"Annie, I've told your boys to throw your beef-cut in with mine again. I'll drive your stuff to the railroad as usual, if it's okay with you—"

She nodded assent almost curtly. "Makin' the drive yerself, Sale?"

"Yes, I'll be on the way by tomorrow morning."

"Ye mean ye'll start off without seein' Glenna?" she demanded.

Surprise at the question stiffened his face. But all he said was: "I'm afraid there won't be time for that—"

"Nonsense!" Annie exclaimed. "I know she's

208

expectin' ye, because she said as much . . . Don't be a knothead, now! Ride over an' see the lass today. Ye've plenty of time!"

He started to shake his head; but before he could make his refusal final, Annie moved off as though she had just remembered something. Hardesty stood undecided, pondering. Should he follow her advice and drop in on Glenna? He cast about in his mind for some necessity which would give him an excuse for visiting the store in MacKinney.

But in the end he threw excuses aside and rode in to town boldly. Glenna was in the store when he arrived.

"Hello, Salem," she greeted him quietly, with no reference whatever to his long absence. "Is the round-up over?"

He said it was, and told her about it, adding that his own calf increase this year had exceeded even his hopes. Glenna listened politely. There was even a faint disinterest in her manner, which distressed him. He broke off: "Will you be going to Sidney this spring, Glenna?"

"No—" There was not even hesitation in her answer. "I can get anything I want freighted in now without going after it. I probably won't make as many trips any more as I used to."

Hardesty's brows lifted. He felt that in her coolness he was fighting something intangible and baffling. It was almost as though she had been waiting, primed for his every friendly advance. Yet he tried once more:

"Perhaps there's some errand or other I can do for you while I'm in Sidney?"

She smiled faintly. "Thank you, Salem. Lieutenant Dodd stopped by yesterday, on his way out on military business. I gave him my list."

Over Hardesty there came again the conviction that she no longer had an interest in him, that she found it in her heart to dislike him even. But why? At a loss to find the answer to that problem, he had no doubt whatever of where he stood with the girl. Whatever chance he had once had with her, it was gone now.

"Well," he said awkwardly, "I wish you good luck, Glenna. I'll say good-by now." In a hollow silence, he turned on his heel and walked out of the store. Daylight the following morning found him well started on the drive to Sidney.

CHAPTER FIFTEEN

Rafe Perrine lost no time, on his return from Omaha, in setting about the formation of a county government nor did the fact that a number of stockmen were away, driving their spring beef-cut to market, delay him. While before, all interest in a local government had been confined to discussion, Perrine was empowered to act. He did not hesitate.

When Hardesty returned from the drive to Sidney, three weeks later, it was to find the county organization far advanced. Nor had any spot in it been reserved for him. Hardesty cared little for that, however. Any office holder below Perrine's station as county commissioner would be at his beck and call, and Hardesty had no taste for fighting Perrine from below.

He stuck to his ranch and plunged into the waiting work. There was always plenty to do. Whatever else he had failed to accomplish in this country, Hardesty had made himself almost rich. It was not that he set a higher value on that than on anything else. He made sure he knew pretty accurately what was going on on the range.

Dublin Annie, for all her isolation, always had some odd pieces of news for him, contributed by a passing rider. Gabe Kyle often rode over for an hour or two. Though much older, and of an altogether different stock—Kyle had been a prosperous farmer for years in Illinois—he was perhaps the best friend Hardesty had among the cattlemen on this range. He kept in close touch with the activities in MacKinney.

Thus Hardesty learned of the slow but steady growth of the town. The Black Hills were still going strong as a gold producing country, but the snap had gone out of the rush. Disgruntled miners were already beginning to turn away, and some of them, coming this way, remained in MacKinney to settle there. Several clapboard houses had gone up, with families installed. There was a livery barn at the lower end of town, still more saloons, and some talk of another store.

Despite his determination not to trouble Glenna, Hardesty was always listening for the slightest item of news about the girl. What he expected to hear—that she had married Lieutenant Dodd, that she was leaving the country, or anything else of the sort—he could not have told. Never did he hear the words for which he was secretly waiting: that she would be glad to see him again.

Late in May, Gabe Kyle rode over one day with an announcement for which Hardesty found himself wholly unprepared. Gabe opened up with a long rambling account of county politics, which he followed with unflagging interest and zeal. Then he broke off casually:

"We're 'bout ready fer a general election."

If he hoped to strike fire from Hardesty with the words, he was disappointed. The latter nodded inattentively, busy with the cigaret he was rolling.

"Runnin' for office, Gabe?" he inquired.

Kyle had some expectations of being made county treasurer. "Me an' the boys," he proceeded levelly, "was hopin' we could persuade yuh to run fer the legislature."

Hardesty looked up quickly, surprised.

"Do you mean that seriously?"

Gabe assured him he did. A glow suffused Hardesty despite his previous intention of holding aloof from political activity.

"That's mighty decent of you—" he began.

Whatever Gabe read in his manner, he broke in: "Don't say no, Hardesty! Think it over before yuh say a word . . . Yo're a big stock grower, now. Men respect yuh. We got to have a good man to represent our district in Lincoln; there ain't nobody who'd satisfy us better'n you."

It was brought to Hardesty forcibly that he was not without backing on this range. He had never sought it, true; for that reason his position was all the stronger. But that men looked up to him was a thought which had never occurred to him before.

"I don't have to think it over," he made answer

slowly. "Bein' a legislator was the farthest from my mind; but if the ranchers want me to run, why I'll say yes."

Kyle approved his decision warmly. So keen was his enthusiasm that he plunged at once into plans for some sort of campaign. But Hardesty was thinking of other things.

"What does Rafe Perrine say about this?" he queried. "Does he know about it?"

"Yes—" Gabe hesitated. "I'll have to admit yo're not just the man Perrine wants."

The fact was not displeasing to Hardesty. "Has he picked a candidate?"

Gabe nodded. "He favors Henry Moran . . . Perrine's backin' is powerful, too. Yuh might as well git used to the idea of that, Hardesty—"

The latter smiled. "I won't let it worry me," he promised.

At Kyle's suggestion, he rode to town the following day. It was the beginning of a busy period for him. With the announcement of his candidature, men made plain that they expected him to do something for himself. Hardesty was content with that. It was his full intention, if he went into this thing at all, to do his best all the way.

He ran into Perrine one day in Henderson's Hotel bar. Rafe had not changed, unless by the addition of an even more confident bearing. He walked over to Hardesty with an almost benevolent smile, but did not make the mistake of attempting to shake hands.

"I understand yo're givin' me a little competition, Hardesty," he opened up pleasantly. Hardesty's brows rose.

"How's that, Perrine?"

Rafe referred to his legislative candidacy deprecatingly. Hardesty shrugged.

"I don't know anything about that," he said dryly. "A number of my friends have expressed a desire for me to represent 'em in the legislature. I've accommodated for that reason."

"I see." Perrine was suavely inscrutable. He laughed easily: "Well, I'll endeavor to give yuh all the trouble I can. May the best man win, Hardesty; he usually does."

The chief element of surprise in this meeting for Hardesty was the fact that Perrine had omitted to sneer at his pretentions. He was unable to decide whether it had any significance, but of one thing he was sure.

"Perrine's changed," he mused soberly. "He's a whole lot keener than when he was sellin' rotgut and Spencers to the Sioux. He'll bear a close watchin'."

As for Perrine's candidate, Moran, Hardesty came into contact with him more often. Moran was a stout, florid man, loud of manner and facile with promises. He was a recent newcomer to this range, and there were those who suggested uncharitably that he was essentially an opportunist.

While Moran was transparent to the sober-minded, he made free consistently with his cigars and drinks, and there were always those who were willing to listen to him. Perhaps with Perrine's help he might manage to scrape together a respectable following. And yet, Hardesty was reasonably confident of his ability to defeat the man at the polls.

Lone Benton took a hand in the campaign in his own manner. One day he came back to the 6 Lightning with the information that he had spent several hours in Moran's company. Hardesty looked at him askance.

"You didn't have your eyes on his cigars, by any chance?" he queried dryly.

Lone grinned. "Wal, I got half a dozen of 'em yere fer the boys." His chief concern, however, had been with Moran's election arguments. He explained them in detail.

Hardesty was not long in deciding that whatever he was, Henry Moran was an experienced politician. He knew all the old dodges and telling gestures. There was just one thing the man had overlooked: he had forgotten that talk, and talk alone, was not the thing on which the men of this range judged a candidate's fitness for office.

Hardesty's campaigning kept him in MacKinney considerably more than usual. It

216

had been his habit to ride to town and return to the ranch the same day, a practice which gave him little enough time there, since the ride each way required several hours. Now he put up at Henderson's Hotel and remained for several days at a time.

Inevitably he saw Glenna. The girl was friendly enough, but always in her manner was the note of faint disinterest. Not again did she invite him into her home, and she was always ready to abandon him when a new customer entered the store. Hardesty could not forego watching her soberly from a distance; he knew what she was doing much of the time, and how little it appeared to mean to her that he was about.

Annie Breen still rode in occasionally to visit the girl. But Annie had been discouraged by the poor results of her efforts from taking further action in the matter. Everything she had done had only widened the breach between Hardesty and the girl. With secret self-reproach, she refrained from urging Glenna, but it did not prevent her from talking endlessly about Hardesty. His political ambitions were a fruitful topic. Annie dilated by the hour on his chances, nor did she allow Glenna to forget that success for him at election meant that he would be leaving the country. She even pretended to confidential information to the effect that Hardesty was seriously considering selling the 6 Lightning, if he won.

Glenna received the news quietly. Not by word or sign did she reveal that such an eventuality meant anything to her. Annie threw up her hands at that. Unconsciously she had been trying to get at the girl from still another angle; now she confessed herself defeated at every turn.

For relief, Annie turned the guns of her indignation on Rafe Perrine. She insisted that he had never changed from what he had originally been.

"Ye can't tell me he'll be sorry to see Hardesty leave this country," she declared forcefully. "Sale is the one man who's stood in his path from the beginnin'; he knows Sale'll come at him the minute he gits out of line! I wouldn't put it past the rapscallion to push Sale into the legislature without his knowin', jest to git rid of him!"

Glenna hearkened thoughtfully. But it was difficult to get out of her what she thought on some subjects. This was one of them. From the time of Abe Slater's death, she had maintained an unbreakable reserve toward the subject of Perrine's misdeeds. She did not alter her rule now for Annie's sake.

But the Irishwoman's words clung in her mind long after they were spoken. Actually, her distrust of Rafe Perrine was as deep as it had ever been. It was based less on reason than on intuition; and Glenna had never yet found occasion to doubt the accuracy of her intuition where matters of this magnitude were concerned.

She began to take an interest in the election. It was not more than a couple of weeks off now. The campaigning was going full swing. To Glenna, so long as she asked for it, there came any amount of political information. Men who sought to impress her, dropping in the store for a plug of tobacco or an order of supplies, and remaining to talk, said things for the pleasure of witnessing her surprise, which they would not otherwise have been persuaded to put into words.

Glenna listened, and held her counsel. But meanwhile she was becoming cognizant of a condition which gave her no little concern. It was not long before she reached the reluctant conclusion that she must do something about it.

One evening, Hardesty was walking past the store, tired and dusty, after leaving his bronc at the livery, when he was astonished to hear his name called in a low, breathless tone. Whirling, he saw Glenna.

"Can you come in a moment?" she faltered. He complied with alacrity, feeling as if he trod on air—or at least on very uncertain ground. The girl did not stop in the store. "We'll go into the house," she murmured; he followed her on to the comfortable living quarters behind the store.

Once there, she turned in the light of the coal oil lamp to study his face earnestly. "Salem, I have learned something which I think you should know." She spoke quietly and steadily, nor did the change in her whole attitude toward him escape Hardesty's attention.

"Yes, Glenna?" He thought his own voice sounded less steady.

"Rafe Perrine is secretly working for your election," she told him.

His jaw dropped. There could be no question that the information came like a bombshell.

"Can you be sure of that?" he asked.

She told him she was. She repeated what she had heard from several different quarters: that Perrine was undermining Moran's standing, without the latter's knowledge. Nothing had been said of Perrine's reason for this double-dealing, but Annie Breen's words had supplied the girl with all the explanation she needed.

"Perrine hopes to get you out of his way," she declared her conviction. "If there have been times when I doubted his purpose, Salem, it is so no longer. He could have no other reason for favoring you. He is afraid that if you learn what he is doing, you will change your mind."

"I'm sure obliged to you, Glenna," Hardesty said huskily. "If it wasn't for you, I'd never've learned this in time—"

"Then you believe me?" she exclaimed quickly.

He showed his own surprise at the question.

"Of course. The only question in my mind is whether I can put a stop to this."

"What will you do?" she asked.

"I'll withdraw my name from the ballot," he said without hesitation. "If Perrine is waitin' till I'm safely gone before he starts his game, he'll have a long wait!"

She could not doubt that he meant what he said. The knowledge sobered her.

"I hope I've done right," she said. "You are needed in the legislature, Salem. But perhaps you are needed here more."

The utter change in her from what she had been so long, emboldened him to say what he did. "Needed or not, here is where I stay while Rafe Perrine is on the loose . . . It's you I'm thinkin' of, Glenna, more than myself."

"I know you think for me, Salem." Her voice was small. There was something electric in the moment. Hardesty's muscles tightened, hope running through him like fire. Before he could take the step forward that would bring him close to her, Glenna turned away quickly. The next moment, she turned the conversation to a safer topic.

Hardesty's face fell slightly. He could not tell whether it was Lieutenant Dodd who had stepped between them once more, or not. But certainly Glenna showed him more warmth than she had done for long. He was humbly grateful for that much.

"I won't forget this," he promised her, making ready to leave. "There was no reason why you needed to tell me what you learned about Perrine; yet you did. It was mighty fine of you, Glenna."

Despite her rigid self-control, she flushed with pleasure. She had never sought to disguise to herself the fact that his approval meant a lot.

"It's nothing, Salem," she assured him. "I hope I will always be ready to do as much . . . I am sure of it," she amended.

The words sent him away with a warm glow where for so long there had existed only the dull, leaden sense of loneliness.

The first person he sought out was the clerk whom Perrine had hired to look after county affairs. To him Hardesty announced that his name was to be taken off the election ballot, and that the fact was to be announced publicly. It was not a matter of indecision with him, he declared; he had made up his mind fully.

Next Hardesty went to Gabe Kyle and told him it was no longer his intention to run for the legislature. Kyle was aghast.

"But why, Sale?" he demanded. "What happened? What's yore reason fer this switch?"

Hardesty could not tell him without tipping his hand. He had no expectation of doing that. He shook his head.

"I can't tell you, Gabe. But that's the way she stands, and you'll have to make the best of it."

Kyle argued long and vigorously without succeeding in moving Hardesty in the slightest. He gave over at length.

"Wal, if that's the way yuh feel about it, we'll jest have to put up another candidate an' elect him," he said stiffly. Hardesty nodded woodenly.

"You do that; and I'll work as hard for his election as anybody," he promised.

A new candidate to fill Hardesty's place was named at a special caucus of the Stockmen's Association the following day. To Gabe Kyle's surprise, he received the nomination himself. There was every reason to believe he would prove a popular candidate. He was well liked, and of his forthrightness and sincerity there was no doubt whatever.

Hardesty grunted his relief on hearing the news. He did not allow the matter to drop with that, either. No opportunity was lost to say a good word for Gabe.

It was two days later before he ran into Rafe Perrine, even though he had been seeking the other. Perrine knew what had been happening; his rocky visage went blank as they met, and there was a hint of steel in his glance.

"I hear yuh decided to withdraw from the race while there's time, Hardesty," he remarked colorlessly. Hardesty pushed close and looked him squarely in the eye.

"Maybe you can guess why," he said flatly. At Perrine's pretense of incomprehension, he shook his head. "It won't work, Perrine. I know your game! You thought you'd ship me safely off to Lincoln, out of your way; but if you ever get rid of me, you sneakin' sidewinder, it won't be that way!"

Perrine's eyes flared up intolerantly. Then he caught himself.

"I don't know what yo're talkin' about, Hardesty, but that's mighty strong language yo're usin'!"

"If I ever can prove what I know about you," Hardesty retorted, "I won't let it go with talk! I aim to be right here handy, where I can go into action!"

He was as good as his word. For when election drew near and passed, it was Gabe Kyle who defeated Perrine's candidate, and a few days later started off for Lincoln and his seat in the legislature. Hardesty was in town to follow the returns, and it was on the street there that Perrine saw him through the window of the sheriff's office, with the taste of defeat fresh in Rafe's mouth.

"There's Hardesty now, damn his hide!" he growled to Pawnee vindictively. "Except for him, I'd have made sure Moran got the election. Now we're out in the cold all around—an' we ain't even got rid of that damned gadfly!"

If Pawnee said nothing, it was not because he did not share Perrine's secret hatred and fear of Hardesty. He did. But understanding Rafe's mental processes thoroughly, he waited for what was to come next. He was not disappointed.

"We've got to get rid of Hardesty some way," Rafe jerked out. "I've had my try—and there he is, still around . . ."

A sinister eagerness crept into Pawnee's features. "Yuh mean fer me to give it a whirl, see what I kin do?" he demanded. Perrine's nod was curt.

"It's yore turn. Pawnee. And I don't mean for monkeyin' around either. Turn yore wolf loose!"

"Don't worry." Pawnee was grimly self-confident. "I'll go after Mister Salem Hardesty in short order. An' when I go after a gent, it ain't long before I finish him!" Perrine knew it for no boast. The fact left him unmoved, however.

"Just see that yuh do," he muttered.

CHAPTER SIXTEEN

The summer season that year was exceptionally dry; no rain fell for two months. The buffalo grass lying in exposed places began to brown early, and even the pine trees lost their gloss. Hardesty found no occasion for worry, however. With his 6 Lightning range enclosed on either side by a river, there was always enough water for his stock.

The time came when it was driven home to him that lack of water was not the only danger with which he might be threatened. One morning he rose to find the sun a blood-red metal ingot in the sky and the air tinged with a sour haze of smoke.

Lone Benton shared his anxiety, stamping his boots on in a hurry and coming into the yard for a look around. "Range is on fire somewheres," he muttered.

The fact that it was miles away made neither Lone nor Hardesty any easier in mind. The latter said: "Better get the boys out. If the fire's off our range, the White and the Niobrara'll save us. If not—" He broke off.

Without bothering to delay for breakfast, the outfit pulled away a few minutes later. Hardesty went with the others. They headed northeast. The pine-clothed ridges made it difficult to see for any distance, but it escaped none of them that the smoke increased in density as they proceeded.

Five miles from the ranch, Hardesty rode up a ridge from the crest of which he saw, far beyond, the fierce, wide-flung wall of advancing flames. It was on his range all right. Even from this distance he could spot small bunches of wildly fleeing steers, hear the low, ominous mutter and crackle of the conflagration.

"Good God!" burst from Pony Johnson as he and the others drew up beside Hardesty. "Why, that's wipin' the heart out of our best range!"

It was true. Although clump after clump of pines went up in smoke like armfuls of roman candles, the fire was also sweeping park after park of rich, valuable range grass. The dryness of the season had left the grass ready for this holocaust. The flames ran through it with the speed of a galloping horse. The steady rain of cinders, riding the wind, threatened the range for half a mile ahead of the advancing wall.

Hardesty whipped out: "Spread out, and get up as close to it as you dare! Our only hope is in back-fires!"

They knew he was right. Left to itself, the fire would sweep the 6 Lightning from end to end; and as for Hardesty's stock, there would not be enough of it left with which to start over.

Ignoring their danger, they shoved forward as

227

fast as the terrified broncs would permit. When they had got so close that the heat stung their skin and crisped their hair, Hardesty called a halt. Swinging out of the saddle, he dared not let go of his horse's bridle. Breaking off pieces of brush, he lit them and started his backfire. Lone and the punchers followed suit.

They had to work in feverish haste. Momentarily the wall of flames threatened to sweep forward and engulf them. The wind was just right. The smoke nearly suffocated Hardesty; it was so thick that the kerchief over his mouth and nostrils was as nothing.

Madly he worked to spread the back-fire. It caught hold with heart-breaking slowness. The flames had to be stamped out of the grass. Once, with his sixgun, Hardesty mercifully knocked over a racing jack-rabbit, its entire coat ablaze, just as it threatened to touch off a patch of range behind him, by dodging past and seeking refuge vainly in the unburned area.

It was Lone who, a few hundred yards away, received sudden warning of their danger. A veritable cloud of blazing brands swept down over him. He threw down his torch before he had half-finished setting his back-fire. The next instant he was slapping at his clothes where they began to smolder in half a dozen places. It was all he could do to hang on to his plunging bronc. Somehow he managed to swing aboard.

A rake of the spurs sent the pony racing toward Hardesty's position.

"Git outa this!" the Texan yelled. "My God, Sale—we'll be burned alive! Git on yore bronc an' run fer it!"

Hardesty knew he was right. It was a bitter pill for him, for he knew they had not succeeded in their object. The best they could hope for was that the partial back-fire would delay the advancing flames long enough to allow them to ride to safety.

Hardesty had a glimpse of the others fleeing destruction. The fire was traveling faster than anyone had quite suspected. Yet he refused to accept defeat. Putting half a mile behind him at the best speed his bronc had to offer, he indicated by waving his arms that they were to attempt a second back-fire.

This time he had chosen a brush-covered swell, where the flames caught quickly. In a few short minutes Hardesty had a long line of fire creeping back to meet the oncoming monster. A glance told him the others had been as successful. Hope leaped in him then. As near as he could estimate, a quarter of his best range had already been destroyed, but if the fire could be checked here, there would still be a chance.

Swiftly the back-fires gathered headway, crawled together in one long blaze, and bounded forward. The heat from it, and from the run-away fire beyond, was terrific. Hardesty felt his skin crack. His lips were raw, his eyes stinging.

"Get back!" he cried. "We've done all we can do here!"

They fell back just in time. With a roar of ferocity, the double wall of flames joined on the crest of the swell. A curling wave of fire sprang sixty feet in the air. A cloud of blazing cinders spewed upward and swept forward on the wind, most of which, however, flickered out before they came raining down. The few that were still burning the 6 Lightning stamped out in a hurry.

They had succeeded in checking the range-fire at this point, but unfortunately for them, the brush they had touched off did not extend across the entire face of the conflagration. A mile to the west, the flames were still working forward; a thick clump of pines went up with a roaring crackle even as Hardesty headed that way.

"We've got to choke that down before all our work goes for nothing!" he jerked out. "Come on, boys—"

Soot-blackened, half-blinded with smoke, and with half of his hair singed off by the heat, he led the way. Swiftly they set about repeating their success with the back-fire. But it was three hours later and a dozen square miles of range lay blackened and useless, before the last embers of the fire were stamped out. The men were so weary they could scarcely stand.

"Let's hope that don't happen ag'in in a hurry!" Rusty Gallup expressed fervently the feelings of them all. Lone, however, was not inclined to let it go at that.

"Question is, how come it happened this time," he growled crustily. "If there'd been a storm, that'd be one thing; but fires don't jest happen!"

The same thought had come to Hardesty, nor could he put out of his mind the suspicion that the fire had been set.

"We'll get back to the ranch now and look after ourselves," he said. "This afternoon we'll have a look around and see what we can find out."

They did as he said. Kezzy Sparrow soon had a hot meal for them, and lard for their burns. In the afternoon, catching up fresh mounts, they set out to seek the mysterious origin of the fire. They had no success. Hardesty spotted the carcasses of two or three 6 Lightning steers who had been caught by the fire and burned to a crisp, but of evidence concerning its cause there was none.

Lone shook his head at that. "It don't mean a thing," he argued. "Any skunk who'd do a thing like that would be mighty careful to cover his trail!"

Hardesty, for one, agreed with him. He held aloof, however, while the Texans discussed the matter, believing he could place the blame accurately enough. Still fresh in his mind was his last encounter with Rafe Perrine. While Rafe would be sure that no direct connection between him and the fire was left behind, Hardesty had no doubt that he knew plenty about it.

Kink Withers, Gabe Kyle's foreman, rode over to talk with Hardesty the following day. "I seen the smoke rollin', yesterday," he said. "What was it, anyway?"

Hardesty told him. Withers's leathery features went sober. "That's bad," he murmured. "Looks like we're in fer a hard luck spell—"

"How's that?"

Withers lowered his voice. "I've lost mebby two dozen head of steers in the last month," he revealed. "How 'bout yoreself?"

"None, yet—that I know of," Hardesty answered. While he was scarcely surprised by the news, it gave him food for thought. "Have you seen anything?"

"Yuh mean the rustlers?" Kink shook his head. "They're mighty careful, whoever they are. We ain't got a thing to go on. It's why I come to talk it over with you."

"Do you know if any of the other outfits are being raided?"

"Mart Pincher thinks he's lost a few head. I dunno 'bout the rest—"

They talked it over at length. Hardesty looked at the matter from every angle before he expressed his mind.

"Keep a close watch from now on, Withers,"

he counseled finally, "and I'll do the same. This must be the same bunch that was gettin' into us last year. They'll have to be brought up short or we'll all go under . . . Meanwhile, if there's anything I can do to help yuh, let me know."

Withers thanked him. "I'll do that, Hardesty. An' you do the same."

He rode away a few minutes later.

Hardesty did not forget the matter. Advising Lone and the others of what he had learned, he suggested a close watch on the range for a time. If the rustlers had not given the 6 Lightning their attention as yet, it could be only a matter of time before they got around to it.

A night guard was set. For three moonlit nights nothing happened. On the fourth night, which was cloudy, Hardesty seemed to have been dozing only a short time when the faint crack of a shot, drifting from afar, jerked him wide awake in a flash. A bound took him to the door, where he anxiously tested the night. The firing came again. There was an urgency in it that told him more than enough.

"Roll out!" he cried sharply. "That's Red, firin' a warnin' signal!"

The others came out of their bunks with a rush. Ten minutes saw them dressed and tossing saddles on their broncs. Before they swung out of the yard, Red Tyler, who had been on night guard, came racing up.

"They're into our stuff!" he jerked out. " 'Bout four of 'em, near's I could tell. They've started to shove a bunch south."

Hardesty and the punchers waited for no more. Within a few minutes they reached the spot where Tyler said the rustlers had been at work. While it was not possible to read sign, their inevitable course was plain. They were pushing the stolen stock toward the gap in the white cliffs across the Niobrara through which Pawnee Failes had once sought to drive his herd onto Hardesty's range.

Half an hour later the crew crossed the river and headed into the gap.

"There they are!" Lone exclaimed harshly. "Makin' fer the sand hills tight as they kin go!"

They soon drew up. That the rustlers knew they were being pursued was evident from the rattle of shots which warned against closing in too carelessly. It meant little to the 6 Lightning. On they rode, relentlessly.

Hardesty drew a bead on one shadowy form and fired. There was an answering yell, and the rustler started away at top speed. A few seconds, and his companions followed on the run.

"Nab them!" Hardesty broke out. "Smoke 'em down if you have to! We're puttin' an end to this!"

But the darkness was against them. A short time sufficed to indicate that the renegades had got away. Ill-pleased as he was, Hardesty reflected that prompt action at least had saved his steers. There were eight or ten in the bunch. They were driven back on the 6 Lightning range.

Hardesty found plenty to think about on the way back to the spread. Insignificant as the raid might appear, taken in connection with the other losses beginning to be reported, there could be little doubt that wholesale rustling had come to harry the range.

Nor was he mistaken. The raid announced by Gabe Kyle's foreman a few days ago was the fore-runner of a systematic series of depredations. Whoever they were, the rustlers proved themselves bold beyond belief. In this day of sparse settlement, they had any amount of wild country in which to hide. Riding out of their retreat, they struck again and again.

Pawnee Failes was soon swamped with more work than he could handle. Two deputies were appointed, but even that did no good. The lawmen rode day and night, without getting anywhere.

It was Mart Pincher's crew who nabbed three men on the range during a raid. They were well known—idlers of low repute, who hung around the saloons in town. Pincher's men had cornered them within half a mile of a bunch of stolen steers. Though they claimed to know nothing about the matter, they were handed over to the sheriff. Within a fortnight they were brought to trial.

Hardesty made a point of being present when the case came up. Court was held in the new schoolhouse which had been built in MacKinney. It was crowded with stockmen, and the circuit judge presided.

A roar of wrath went up when the three renegades were acquitted for lack of evidence. But nothing could be done about it. As had been the case on the southern ranges, it was virtually impossible to prove a case of rustling.

The same thing happened less than a month later. This time it was two men whom Hardesty's crew nabbed on the border of the 6 Lightning range. Against Lone Benton's advice, Hardesty saw them turned over to the law. Ten days later they were free. They walked out of the court room with so insolent an air that Hardesty suspected the rustlers were laughing at him and the other stockmen.

Still the raids went on. Not even Annie Breen was immune. It infuriated Lone to see her despoiled of her few head of steers; he was busy riding her range on Ghost Creek almost as much as he was the 6 Lightning. Hardesty said nothing. Nor was he surprised when, late in the summer, Lone came to him one day with the announcement that he was going to leave.

"You mean—you're quittin' your job, Lone?"

Benton nodded sheepishly. "Me an' Annie are goin' to ride to town an' get spliced," he explained. His ire rose then. "It ain't fair—her bein' alone like she is! Them hombres she's got workin' fer her don't amount to shucks. She needs a man to look after 'er, an' I aim to do it!"

Hardesty nodded his comprehension. "I'll be sorry to lose you, Lone. But I think you're doin' the right thing. Annie'll make you a good wife. And it ain't as if we wouldn't see each other any time we want . . . Good luck to you both."

He rode to town the day Lone and Annie were married, and attended the ceremony. Glenna was there also. Hardesty half-expected Lieutenant Dodd to appear, but he did not. The girl gave a wedding supper in her home behind the store, after which Lone and Annie, a Breen no longer, set out once more for Ghost Creek.

Less than a week later, a third trial for rustling came up. It followed the precedent of the others; the three men charged with throwing a long rope on some of Lone and Annie's Tomahawk steers were discharged as usual for lack of proof.

When the trial broke up, word spread that a cattlemen's meeting was called for the same night. Feeling ran high, and it was understood that some definite action was to be decided on.

Hardesty attended, with Rusty Gallup, whom he had made his new foreman. The session was a warm one. The burden of the stockmen was that the law had proven helpless. They must take matters into their own hands if they were to get anywhere.

Lone Benton was present, crisp and fiery. "I move we forget about arrestin' these coyotes," was his contribution. "Hangin' is what they need. God knows they're askin' fer it! That way we'll be gittin' results—"

A chorus of agreement arose from the others. Not a man here but was primed and ready for stern measures. Even Hardesty agreed that they must do different from what they had been doing in the past. The meeting broke up on that note. Men did not talk freely about hanging, even where they knew their words would go no farther; but as he headed back for his ranch, Hardesty knew what would follow when rustlers were nabbed another time. He was ready to play his part if he should be among the captors.

If Rafe Perrine had any thoughts on recent happenings, he kept them to himself. Hardesty knew, because he took care to check up on Perrine's movements. Rafe might be playing his own game, but he was keeping well under cover.

One morning early in September, Hardesty was enjoying an after-breakfast smoke in the ranch yard when the sound of hoofs turned him. For a moment he stared, frozen. Then venting an exclamation, he sprang forward as Pony Johnson's bronc jogged up with Pony sprawled, limp and apparently lifeless, across the saddle.

Hardesty got the puncher to the ground. His yell brought Gallup and the others. They looked Johnson over. He had been bored through the shoulder, but not fatally. Hardesty forced some whisky down his throat, but it was half an hour before Pony was able to tell his story.

"Happened—over on the—White," he gasped then. "I jumped a couple rustlers. Hard. They . . . had a calf down. There was a brandin' fire—"

"Who were they?" Hardesty bit off.

Johnson shook his head weakly. "I couldn't— make out. Light was too weak . . . They seen me an' took out," he managed. "I followed. But they was too slick fer me, I expect. They—"

"Bushwhacked yuh. Is that it?" Rusty interposed gruffly.

Pony nodded. Chagrin showed in his eyes. "It was either them or me, an' they held all the aces!"

"Never mind." Hardesty clipped the words off grimly. "They got away with it this time. But we'll go after 'em, and if we catch up, it'll be a different story!"

CHAPTER SEVENTEEN

But they never did catch up. Late that afternoon Hardesty and the others had to confess themselves defeated once more. The calf the rustlers had tied up was located; but Pony Johnson had appeared on the scene so early that there was no telltale brand to be read. Hardesty turned back with slow-gathering wrath burning in his heart.

Red Tyler rode to Fort Robinson and returned with the army physician. He doctored Pony up, warning him he would have to spend some time on his back. The Texan assented, tight-lipped. Afterward the doctor had a few words with Hardesty down at the corrals.

"You have no idea who is responsible for these raids?" he queried. Hardesty delayed over his answer.

"If I could be sure, I'd do somethin' about it in a hurry," he said at length, and added: "Whoever it is, I'd almost as soon still be dealin' with the Sioux."

The medico nodded. "I've seen this same condition rise on more than one frontier. It seems to follow inevitably the opening of a new country. Let's hope you can put a stop to it before too long."

"It'll get worse before it gets any better," Hardesty predicted.

Nor was he mistaken. During the following fortnight, rustlers harried the range like a veritable plague of locusts. So many raids were reported that it seemed incredible only one gang was responsible. Mart Pincher, of the Circle P, announced that in three nights he had lost over forty head.

The 6 Lightning was busier maintaining a night guard than they were ordinarily with their daily work. Even so, Hardesty knew the renegades were getting into him deep. A few steers now, and a few later, driven from isolated portions of the range, soon counted up. On his infrequent visits to MacKinney, Hardesty kept a serene countenance, but to Lone Benton he confessed himself worried.

"If it keeps up the way it's goin', I'll wind up in a jam," he declared soberly.

Lone himself was in no better case. His and Annie's smaller herd had suffered heavy losses in the comparatively short period since the rustling had started up again.

"I reckon yuh know where to look to place the blame," he said bluntly. Hardesty understood him completely, but he found the other's tone suggestive.

"What do you mean?"

"Has it occurred to yuh that most of this dirty

work has been pulled since election?" Lone demanded shrewdly.

The circumstance had not escaped Hardesty. He nodded.

"Perrine'd do anythin' to smash yuh," Lone stated his conviction flatly. "Since he couldn't git rid of yuh any other way—"

Hardesty knew he was right. He had already come to this same conclusion. He said as much.

"An' don't forget that Perrine made Pawnee Failes sheriff," the grizzled Texan continued thinly. "That wa'n't no accident. Sale! They're still birds of a feather . . . Perrine's covered hisself mighty slick, but he don't fool me a second. That buzzard's crooked as a corkscrew— he's gettin' his cut of every steer that goes down the gulch with a phony brand on its hip!"

Not even this vehement declaration fetched a demur from Hardesty. He said: "You can't bring a charge like that against a man and hope to make it stick, without plenty of proof."

"There yuh go—thinkin' about the law ag'in," Lone burst out disgustedly. "If you'd a took matters in yore own hands years ago, the way I wanted yuh to, there wouldn't be no Perrine to bother us now—or no Pawnee Failes either!"

"You mean you think we should go after 'em now?"

Lone's features reddened. "What yuh think I been talkin' about?" he exclaimed testily. "What's all this red tape an' legal foolishness amount to, anyway? We both know Perrine's as guilty as hell! There's only one cure fer his kind. That's an external application uh rawhide rope, an' keepin' his feet high!"

Hardesty thought it over momentarily, and shook his head. "Perrine and Failes both deserve hangin'," he said. "But we won't go that far just yet." Lone tried to argue the matter with him, but he was adamant.

"Give 'em enough rope, and they'll save us the trouble by hangin' themselves," he said.

Lone grunted impatiently. "Lot uh good that'll do, if they've got us hung goose high before that happens," he grumbled. But he declared himself ready for any measures against the renegades which Hardesty suggested.

"Good," the latter nodded. "You're keepin' a strict watch on Ghost Creek, I take it?"

"I'll say I am!"

"You do that," Hardesty agreed, "and hold yourself ready. If I spot anything, I'll give you a call."

Hardesty swung his bronc and started away. They had met on the trail a few miles from Ghost Creek; Benton headed back there, while Hardesty made for the 6 Lightning once more.

Half a mile from the ranch he saw that something was going on. A couple of the boys were getting up broncs in a hurry—Red Tyler and Rusty, that was. Pony, who had got on his feet once more, stood near the house. Even at this distance his plaintive voice could be heard, if not the words. Hardesty shoved forward.

His foreman came to meet him as he drew near. Hardesty read that in his face which spelled trouble.

"What is it, Rusty?"

"More of the same!" Gallup bit off grimly. He added the terse explanation: "I ran acrost a small brandin' fire down on the Niobrara this mornin'! It's only a day or so old!"

Hardesty read the significance of this at a glance. He barked: "On this side of the river?"

"No, half a mile to the south, it was."

Hardesty nodded, thinking. His stock drifted off its own range occasionally; it was impossible to avoid. Sometimes he thought the steers were helped to drift. As close a watch could not be kept over the outlying portions of rough country, and it would have been easy for brand blotters to do their work there without particular danger of detection.

"Spot any sign?" he queried.

"Not handy. I didn't waste any time."

Hardesty nodded. "We'll get over there right away."

Red was ready to join them. Pony Johnson called: "Mebby I better ride 'long with yuh, Hard—"

Hardesty paused. He knew how the puncher's wound irked him. Pony would have given anything to swing into the hull and turn to the waiting work once more. But Hardesty shook his head.

"You better stick around and take care of that shoulder," he decided. "A mistake now might set you back a couple of weeks—and I need you."

Pony's scowl said that he would have argued the point, given the chance. But Hardesty gave him none. A moment later he, Red and Gallup jogged away from the ranch in the direction of the Niobrara.

The point at which Rusty had discovered the branding fire was over a dozen miles away. They lost no time getting there. The Texan led the way unerringly; Hardesty found the little heap of ashes and charred sticks beside a patch of brush, where a running iron had been heated.

His examination was swift. Getting up from his squatting position beside the ashes, he nodded to Rusty. "Made sometime yesterday," he said. "We'll look around. I'd say it was a yearlin' that was overbranded. I want to see that."

They were unable to locate the steer, however. Probably it had been driven from the vicinity. Nor did they find the sign of the range thief, search though they would. But an hour later, Red Tyler vented a shout which brought the others to him.

Red had discovered the remains of a second branding fire. Hardesty's jaw hardened as he stared down at it.

"By gravy, a little more uh this an' yuh won't have no spread, Hard!" Rusty exclaimed harshly. Hardesty did not answer directly.

"Spread out," he directed curtly. "We're combin' this ridge thoroughly—and the hollows too. Don't miss a one of those coulees. I aim to find out how far this business has gone!"

They did as he directed. Diligent as he was, Hardesty found nothing himself, but Gallup ran across a third branding fire a couple of miles away.

That was the extent of their discoveries. Hardesty was rolling it over grimly, when a hail floating across the brush brought him around.

Kezzy Sparrow, his cook, lanky and tall now in comparison to the gangling, big-jointed youngster whom Hardesty had picked up in Nebraska City on his return from the war, rode forward furiously, waving his arm.

"Come a-runnin'!" he yelled. "Yuh been tolled off. Hard! The stuff's bein' raided over on the White!"

There was more of this, spilling from his lips breathlessly. Hardesty cut him off short. "Tell it so we can understand," he rapped.

Kezzy complied. Unsatisfied with Hardesty's instructions to remain at the ranch, he said,

Pony Johnson had laboriously got up a bronc and headed out on a little pasear of his own. He had not gone far when, coming out on a ridge overlooking the White, to his amazement he had discovered half a dozen men hazing a bunch of thirty or forty steers across the river. Pony had made no mistake this time, striking back at once for the ranch. Once there he instructed the cook to go after Hardesty and the others. Himself, Pony had started out to gather some other ranchers.

Hardesty frowned on hearing that. "Where'd he head?" he asked.

Kez wasn't sure. "I think he was makin' fer Ghost Creek."

"Good!" Hope rang in Hardesty's tone. "With Lone and his boys, we may be able to do somethin'!"

At a word from him, they started across the range for the White. Hardesty consulted the sun anxiously; it rode low in the west, but he estimated that they still had several hours of light. He failed to comment on the fact that the cook rode with them. Kez was armed, and every man of them would be needed.

They saw nothing of anyone until the White was reached. The river valley appeared deceptively quiet. It seemed incredible that rustlers had been active here, until they came across the tracks of a large bunch of steers. These had been driven across the river and into a notch giving upon the rough land to the north.

Staring at the tracks, Hardesty swore under his breath. Pony had made no mistake. There were upwards of forty head in that bunch! It was the boldest steal yet.

Before he could speak, there was a crash of movement in the pines behind him and three horsemen appeared. Hardesty relaxed at sight of Lone Benton and two other men. Lone jogged forward, eyes glinting.

"It come sooner'n yuh expected," he grunted.

"That's right," Hardesty assented.

No more was said. These men knew what lay before them. Without ado they struck across the river and took up the trail of the rustled steers.

The raiders had pushed them hard. Topping the white cliffs above the White, they had disappeared in the rough land beyond. Hardesty followed at a relentless pace, with no thought now of sparing the horses. If they were successful this time, the renegades would stop at nothing. He had no longer any doubt that their single-minded aim was to wipe him out, and it looked like they were in a fair way to doing it.

Within half an hour the trail ran out on stony ground, and the pursuers found themselves slowing up. They hung on doggedly. Mart Pincher and three of his punchers overhauled them. The rancher had received word of the raid. Others were on the way, he said. He had passed the call along.

Hardesty listened inattentively. All his faculties were trained on the matter in hand.

The sun was yet an hour high when the trail struck down a shallow valley in which the tracks were easy to follow. Twenty minutes later the cowmen rode out at the head of the valley. Lone Benton drew rein to raise a pointing finger.

"There's yore steers, Sale!" he exclaimed.

He was right. A mile beyond, the cattle could be seen. The stock thieves were hurrying it along. "Here's our chance to nail those birds dead to rights!" Hardesty jerked out. He led the rush.

The crack of a rifle, while they were still some hundreds of yards to the rear, gave evidence that the rustlers had seen them. They closed in undeterred. The brush here was thick and high, so that little enough could be seen at close range. The red glow cast by the descending sun further deceived the eye. But a moment later Hardesty cried:

"They're on the run! Never mind the steers— we've got to nab those gents!"

The rustlers, half a dozen in number, as Pony Johnson had said, were well aware of their danger. They had given up all hope of hanging on to the stolen 6 Lightning steers, and were making a break in the hope of effecting their escape.

Spreading out, and firing whenever a target

presented itself, the cowmen raced after. They found themselves fighting a long, brush-covered slope across which the quarry fled like scattering quail, clinging low in the saddle and firing backward with deadly persistence. Hardesty heard a slug drone viciously past his head; he saw Lone's bronc unwind as a bullet snarled off the buckle of its headstall.

But they were steadily drawing up. The rustlers saw it. Abruptly they swung down the slope. There were rocks down there, edging the dry creek. They made for cover at a mad pace, but pursuit was hot on their heels now.

Hardesty fired a shot which dropped one of the rustler's broncs. The man was flung a dozen yards. He scrambled to his knees, his hand streaking to his thigh. He still had his six-gun. His beady eyes were fastened on Hardesty.

Before he could get his gun up, Lone fired. The rifle slug crashed into the man's chest at short range. With a cry, he flung up his arms, wheeled around, and fell headlong.

"Much obliged, Lone!" Hardesty didn't even draw in, tossing the words over his shoulder, though he knew that but for the other, it might be he who was lying there.

The rustlers reached the rocks a moment later. The cowmen were so close on their heels that they made no attempt to haul up. Instead, they started to spread out, fleeing in different directions. Two of the rustlers were riding side by side. As they flashed past an opening in the rocks, Hardesty got a look at them. What he saw sent a burst of wrath through him. The sun had dropped below the horizon moments before, he couldn't see very well; and yet, he was sure of the identity of at least one man.

Mart Pincher was near at hand. He had seen the same as Hardesty.

"Pawnee Failes, by God!" he ejaculated.

Hardesty nodded grimly. It was the sheriff, all right. He and his companion disappeared in the brush. Hardesty pounded after, with Pincher close behind, but it appeared Pawnee had shaken them off the trail at last. In the last light of the evening, Hardesty drew rein in the knowledge that they had lost the quarry. He said as much to Pincher.

So hot was the rancher's ire that he was for pushing on till they caught up with the lawman, if it was a day from now, or a week. Hardesty brought him up short.

"We ain't makin' any mistake about this," he declared. "It was Pawnee Failes, right enough, and his crowd from the saloons in town. But if we go there and accuse him, we'll get nowheres!"

"What'll yuh do, then?" Mart demanded. Hardesty reflected.

"If Pawnee rode with this bunch once," he said finally, "he'll do it again. Then is when we'll be

251

ready for him. We'll keep a close watch. He may think he wasn't recognized. But the next time, we'll get him with the goods. It won't do him any good to try to argue out of it!"

When he had cooled off a bit, Pincher agreed that this was the best plan. He shook his head.

"I wouldn't figger Pawnee to have brains 'nough fer this game," he said in a puzzled tone. Hardesty debated naming the man he was sure stood behind Failes, but in the end he desisted. Time enough to uncover Rafe Perrine, once Pawnee was laid by the heels. Meanwhile, he'd play a waiting game.

The other cowmen had taken after the rest of the rustlers. It was an hour after dark before they drifted back, muttering their disappointment. They had had no luck. The raiders had got away clean. Fierceness leaped in their eyes, however, on hearing what Hardesty and Mart Pincher had to tell them.

"By grab, we'll square accounts with this crowd, if that's the way she stacks up!" Lone Benton exclaimed harshly. "We're callin' a meetin' of the boys fer tomorrow! It won't be long before we git some results yuh kin tie to!"

CHAPTER EIGHTEEN

The White River Stockmen's Association gathered the following morning at Hardesty's ranch. It was a stormy meeting. Rage filled the ranchers at the knowledge that the sheriff of the county was mixed up in the rustling of their stock. For the first time Hardesty heard discontented mutterings against Rafe Perrine, though so far it was only because Perrine had appointed Pawnee Failes to office.

Lone Benton would have fired off a blistering comment of his own against Perrine, had not Hardesty stopped him. Plainly the grizzled Texan itched to come out with the truth.

"Take it easy," Hardesty counseled under his breath. "The facts will come out soon enough. It'll make the kick-back against Perrine come all the harder."

Lone subsided, grumbling.

No time was lost about setting a watch over the sheriff's movements. Red Tyler and one of Mart Pincher's punchers were named for the job. Hardesty warned against others taking a hand.

"The way I figure, Pawnee don't know we're onto him," he said. "He's got to go on feelin' that way, if we're goin' to get any results. If he notices too many of our boys around town, he'll be apt to watch his step."

"What about this rustler Lone bumped off las' night?" someone demanded. The dead man had been recognized as a saloon habitue often seen in MacKinney.

"I'll have him taken to town and handed over to Failes," Hardesty answered. "Pawnee knows there was a raid, and he knows we know about it. No point in hidin' anything like that."

It was decided that Tyler and Pincher's man should take the dead rustler to town and turn him over to the sheriff, since it would make a good excuse for them to appear there. They started off a few minutes later, the body tied across an extra bronc. The ranchers dispersed to await the call to action.

Pawnee and a brawny deputy, with a hang-dog look about him, rode out to the 6 Lightning at noon. If Red Tyler and his companion followed, they wisely kept out of sight. Hardesty found it a tax on his endurance to meet the sheriff with a composed face and answer his questions about the rustling quietly. Failes pretended to be investigating the raid; he even managed to simulate anger that these things should continue to go on.

"I'll ride out on the range fer a look around," he told Hardesty ambitiously. "I might find some sign. Can't ever tell what'll lead to somethin'."

"You be damn careful you don't find more than you aim to," Hardesty thought to himself. Aloud, he said: "That's right, Failes. If you find out anything, let me know."

"I'll do that," Pawnee promised, swinging his leg over his saddle. He and his deputy pulled away. Hardesty wanted to follow, but he held himself back, remembering his advice to the other cowmen.

Pawnee did not return that way, but after dark that evening, Red Tyler jogged up for a word with Hardesty. He had not let the sheriff out of his sight all day.

"He rode out to where the rustler was bumped off, an' fooled around a while," Red said. "But mostly it looked to me like he was studyin' the country fer future reference."

Hardesty nodded, lips taut. "He didn't make a phony move all day, I don't suppose?"

"No, he's on his good behavior. But he'll dang soon git tired uh that," Red predicted. "I better shove along, 'fore he gits too far ahead—"

Pausing long enough to get up a fresh bronc, and stuff some food in his saddle-pocket in case of emergency, Tyler departed to continue his vigil.

Though Hardesty held himself ready constantly, no word came for two days. Hardesty made a routine trip to town on the second day. He noted that Pawnee was in his office, and Red Tyler

255

he spotted in Henderson's saloon; but no words passed between them in private, since Rafe Perrine was in the place at the time.

Sparks flew when Rafe and Hardesty exchanged glances. Neither made any pretense of tolerance. But Perrine appeared contemptuous. Probably he felt secure in the belief that a short time would see his enemy ruined, and thus rendered innocuous. Hardesty gave him an angry look and, downing his drink, turned on his heel and left the place.

He had intended stopping to visit Glenna this afternoon. But the thoughts which arose on seeing Perrine had put him in a sour mood. He would be poor company for the girl. Changing his mind, he headed back for the 6 Lightning.

Darkness was scarcely an hour old that night when Mart Pincher's man rode out to the ranch. Hardesty heard him clatter into the yard and went to the door.

"Where's Red?" he demanded.

"Pawnee's crowd is gatherin', Hardesty!" the puncher threw back. "We seen the high sign passed; a lot of shady gents are driftin' out of town. Somethin's up—we dunno where, yet. Red's watchin' the sheriff. He says yo're to pass the word fer the cowmen to gather here right away, an' wait!"

It was enough for Hardesty. Without loss of time he sent Pony, Gallup and Kezzy Sparrow to warn the other ranchers. They were to come to the 6 Lightning immediately, bringing as many men as they could. The Circle P puncher returned to MacKinney to keep in touch with Red.

Within an hour the cowmen began to arrive. It was a grim-faced group that gathered in the kitchen at the 6 Lightning. All were heavily armed. Little was said, however. It was not a time for words.

Towards ten o'clock, Tyler himself pounded into the ranch yard. They were waiting for him.

"Pawnee's bunch is headin' for Pincher's spread," he called out. "Are yuh all ready to ride, Hard?"

Hardesty was. Better than a dozen strong, the cowmen swung into the saddle and started out, with him at their head. Mart Pincher, bristling at this threat to his steers, pushed up beside Hardesty and Red.

"How many men's Failes got with him, Tyler?" he rasped.

Red wasn't certain. "Half a dozen, I judge."

"An' yo're shore they're hittin' fer my place?"

"Wal, Pawnee joined the others a mile out of town, an' they headed up Crazy Creek—"

That settled it. Pincher's Circle P was the only ranch which lay in that direction. Saddle leather creaked and metal clinked on metal as these men struck into a brisker pace. Half an hour saw them on the edge of Pincher's range.

257

Mart was sufficiently familiar with the lay of the land to declare with some accuracy at what point the rustlers were most likely to strike. "There'll be a lot of stuff down in the bottom along the north fork," he muttered. "The rims'll give us a chance to git up close."

It was as he said. From the north branch of Crazy Creek, the land sloped up to ledge-crowned ridges affording excellent cover. However, Hardesty called a halt a mile away. He and Pincher rode on alone. Reaching the ridge, they cautiously scouted the creek bottoms. For a time the starlit range appeared peaceful, tenantless. Then the sodden pound of hoofs came to their ears; there was a low, urgent call through the gloom. Pincher tightened up.

"That's them!" he jerked out lowly. "They're down there, the mangy skunks!"

He and Hardesty pulled away without delay, returning to the waiting posse. Hardesty gave crisp instructions. The cowmen split up, half of them taking each side of the creek, so that when they closed in, the rustlers would be caught within a wall of men.

"Spread out and keep your eyes open," Hardesty warned. "Don't let a man of 'em get away! And most of all, watch for Pawnee. We're makin' a clean sweep this time!"

It was all right with the others.

"I'll fire a double-shot as a signal," were

Hardesty's final words. "When you hear that, wherever you are, go into action."

But he gave the men plenty of time to get into position. He could afford to, since it would take Pawnee's crowd some time to gather the steers they intended to make away with. Apparently they expected to sweep Pincher's range clean. Up from the dusky creekbottom floated the sounds of racing hoofs, the snort of frightened steers. Hardesty was unable to spot anyone with certainty at this distance. It didn't matter.

After a suitable delay, he pushed through a gap in the granite ledge topping the ridge, and started cautiously downward. He soon began to see better. A sizeable bunch of stuff had been gathered and was being held beside the creek. Several men were with them. The rest must be near.

Drawing his gun, Hardesty started to fire and then hesitated. He would have liked to spot Pawnee Failes if possible. But the sheriff must be there. There was no chance for him to get away. Hardesty fired twice.

As the flash of his gun lanced the night, a cry of surprise arose from the rustlers. Jerking their firearms, they blazed away in his direction. But it was only a moment before the cowmen swung into action. Guns cracked from a dozen directions.

Hardesty heard Pawnee's bull voice then. "Pull out of this!" he roared. "The hell with the steers! We're damn near surrounded!"

He was not mistaken. The cowmen had hemmed in this valley with admirable completeness. From every quarter rose their challenging yell or the bark of their weapons as they raced forward. It threw panic into the rustlers. Forgetting the steers utterly, they scattered and started away at a gallop, only to be turned back again and again. Steadily the scope of their movement was narrowed. Hardesty heard a horse scream and then crash down; not far from him, Lone Benton let out a yell of wrath as a slug clipped his ear. Hardesty himself was nearly hit more than once. It made no difference to him. Grimly determined, he made for Pawnee Failes with single-minded purpose, intending to nab the lawman as quickly as possible—take him alive.

Down here in the brush, all was a tangle of confusing shadows. It was difficult to recognize a man even when you were on top of him. A rider loomed up before Hardesty suddenly. The latter leaned forward, peering. It wasn't Pawnee. Hardesty rose in his stirrups and chopped at the other with his gun barrel just as the man fired almost in his face. The shot went wide. Hardesty's blow catching him across the side of the head, the rustler folded out of the saddle like an empty sack.

Yells sounded excitedly a hundred yards away as a renegade sought to break through the cordon. Apparently he was having some success in the attempt. Shots lanced the dark redly; the drum of madly racing hoofs swiftly diminished. A couple of cowmen took after the fugitive.

As for the rest of the stock thieves, they soon found themselves outnumbered. Two chose to shoot it out on the spot; Hardesty saw one blasted off his horse. The second was hit in the arm. He dropped his gun and yelled for mercy.

But there was no mercy in these men. Within two minutes the remaining renegades were taken. There were four who sat their saddles in the center of an ominous ring of cowmen, sullen with fear. One was Pawnee Failes, another the wounded rustler. There had been seven all told. Counting out the dead man, and the man Hardesty had knocked cold, that meant that one of their number had escaped. A minute later, two punchers came pounding back with confirmation of the fact.

Hardesty shoved forward to face Pawnee. "Well, Failes, it looks like the end of your string."

Ready to crack, Pawnee glowered. Suddenly he burst out: "Yo're a dang fool, Hardesty! Here I come out here to nab these birds, an' yuh take me fer one of 'em!"

The other rustlers stared at him, amazed. One guffawed harshly. "None o' that, Pawnee!" he growled. And to Hardesty: "He's one of us, all right. Don't make any mistake about it!"

"We won't," Hardesty assured him briefly.

"What's all the palaver about?" Lone Benton broke in, roughly. "We got a job on our hands here. Let's git it over with!" There were exclamations of assent. Lone and most of the others started to drift toward the clump of cottonwoods farther down the creek.

Hardesty knew well enough what this meant. It sent a chill over him. For as long as he had awaited his vengeance against these men, he had never intended it to go this far. And yet, he knew the temper of his companions too well to attempt to dissuade them. So aroused were they after weeks of persecution that his protests would have done no good.

The man he had knocked out was dragged to his feet and thrust in his saddle. All halted under the trees in grim silence, except for the uneasy muttering of the rustlers. Ropes were tossed over limbs, running nooses adjusted and thrust over their heads.

"Okay—let 'em have it!" Lone grated.

One after another, the rustlers were jerked out of their saddles to hang kicking and twitching. Pawnee was the last to be hauled forward. He broke down as the rope was being placed around his neck.

"Hardesty, fer Gawd's sake!" he pleaded.

"Don't let 'em do this to me! I'll quit the country—I'll do anything yuh say, if you'll let me go!"

Hardesty pushed into the ground. "Hold on, boys! At least we can see what Failes has got to say—"

"Sure! I'll tell yuh anything!" Sweat broke out on Pawnee's beefy face. Plainly he welcomed the chance to talk, brief as it might be.

"Suppose you tell us just how much Rafe Perrine had to do with this rustlin'," Hardesty suggested.

The proposal evoked a murmur of astonishment from the cowmen. "Perrine?" one exclaimed. "What's he got to do with it?" They fell silent then, awaiting Pawnee's answer.

"Perrine's behind all of it!" he declared earnestly. "He aimed to smash yuh, Hardesty— along with Pincher an' some others! He planned all the raids, picked the men who was to make 'em. He even made me sheriff so's we wouldn't have nothin' to worry about from the law—"

A roar of anger arose from the incredulous ranchers. As Pawnee forged on, damning Perrine more definitely with every word, they abandoned all thought that he could be lying. His facts were too circumstantial.

"Perrine!" Mart Pincher ejaculated. "That oily wolf! He had us all fooled, the—"

"Not quite all of us, Pincher," Hardesty struck

in coolly. "I knew this long ago, but I couldn't prove it."

"It's proved now!" Lone rasped harshly. "Come on! Swing Pawnee off, an' we'll go after Perrine!"

The sheriff's throaty gasp was loud. "No, no!" he cried. "Yuh can't do this to me!"

The words were cut off short by the rope which tightened about his scrawny throat before Hardesty had time to do anything about it.

Five minutes later the cowmen were riding toward MacKinney. They expected to find Rafe Perrine there, if he had not been warned already by the rustler who had escaped.

The fear that Perrine had received warning was not unfounded. Even as the first of the rustlers swung into the air at the end of a rope, the one who had escaped raced into MacKinney and flung off his bronc before Henderson's Hotel. A few strides carried him into the bar. Perrine was there.

"Rafe!" the man cried.

His tone was enough to warn Perrine of danger. Swiftly he came forward, thrusting the man outside, fastening a firm grip on his arm.

"Suppose yuh lower yore voice!" he rapped out fiercely. "What do yuh mean by comin' direct to me, anyway?"

"They're onto us!" was the rushing answer.

"It's the cowmen, Rafe—they nailed Pawnee an' the others! I dunno how I managed to git away!"

Tension caught Perrine up at the news. But he did not lose his head.

"Well?" he snapped.

"They'll be comin' for you next!" the rustler told him. "Yuh know what Pawnee is! When they git a rope around his neck, he'll spill the whole business!"

Rafe was afraid it was only too true. What he heard as the other rushed on convinced him. Yet even now he was not inclined to flee. His whole stake, everything he had in the world, was here. He thought swiftly, his face an inscrutable mask. When he spoke it was in an iron tone.

"Curly," he said, "yo're ridin' to Fort Robinson as fast as God'll let yuh. Reach Captain Hanchard. Tell him these cowmen have gone on a tear—that I've barricaded myself in the jail to save myself from a band of armed lynchers! Tell him I want protection from the army—an' damned quick! Got it?"

Curly had. The next moment he was in the saddle and jabbing the steel home. The pony started with a leap. Its rider guided it toward the trail to Fort Robinson. In less than a minute he was gone from sight.

For a moment, Perrine stood where he was, his face grim and hard. Turning on his heel then, he headed for the jail. It was dark tonight, but he found his way inside without trouble. Methodically he locked and barred the doors, dug out the available arms and ammunition, and fell to waiting for whatever was to come.

Truth to tell, Perrine had long expected this hour. He was ready for it. If it came to a bitter showdown with Hardesty and his crowd, Perrine was ready for that too. He was only too anxious to square accounts with his enemy once and for all, and this looked like the best chance he was ever likely to get.

As for Hardesty, he too had waited long for this moment. Riding later into the upper end of MacKinney's street at the head of the cowmen, he asked himself whether Perrine had already fled. He need not have worried. A man ran out from a saloon as the horsemen advanced. He seemed to know what was wanted.

"He's down at the jail, Hardesty!" he called, motioning towards the building.

Hardesty nodded coolly, heading that way. The others began to grow impatient now. They shoved forward. Their number had swelled to more than a score.

It was dark around the jail, with only a lantern burning dimly inside. Yet there seemed to be men gathered about the door. Hardesty peered sharply. The first warning he received that something was wrong, was a curt, military-sounding voice which barked: "Attention! Ready arms!" There was a rattle and click of rifles being cocked.

"What the hell!" Lone Benton ejaculated wrathfully, at Hardesty's side. "What is this?"

Indisposed to delays of any sort, the cowmen would have closed in regardless, but Hardesty halted them. He thought he made out a number of soldiers before the jail, arms ready. The next moment he was sure. A slim, assured young officer stepped out, holding up his hand. It was Lieutenant Dodd.

"Don't come any closer, men!" he warned. "This jail is under military protection, and nothing will happen while we're here." He gathered confidence as the cowmen hesitated. Taking still another step forward, he lowered his voice to conversational pitch.

"What seems to be the trouble, Hardesty?" he asked.

CHAPTER NINETEEN

Gazing at Lieutenant Dodd, Hardesty felt his anger against the man swell sharply. Dodd had already stepped between him and the one woman who meant anything to him. That was bad enough. And now the officer sought to protect his worst enemy from the retribution that was Perrine's just due.

Hardesty did not lose his head, however. He did not need to be warned that there could be no violence used against the United States army. It was a matter of making Lieutenant Dodd see the light. Hardesty said flatly:

"We want Perrine."

If he hoped to jar Dodd to a deeper curiosity with his bluntness, he failed. Dodd responded curtly: "I don't doubt that you do. I was warned you were after him—"

"By Perrine himself, I take it?" Hardesty thrust in thinly. Dodd ignored the implication.

"Just what do you want of him—you cowmen?" he queried.

Every man present was listening with painful alertness, waiting for what was to come. They saw the dilemma in which Perrine's quick action in summoning the military had landed them.

But they were not inclined to be cheated of their vengeance.

The storm of harsh accusations against Perrine, from a dozen throats, almost drowned out Hardesty's answer to the officer's question. Dodd showed annoyance, but Hardesty waited for quiet and then said:

"Perrine's a renegade. He's been directing the rustlers who've been runnin' us ragged! Don't make any mistake about this business, Dodd—*we know!*"

"Maybe you'd like to say how you know," Dodd came back at him dryly. "What's your proof, Hardesty?"

It effectually silenced the latter for the moment. He was too wary to repeat Pawnee Failes's confession just before he was hanged. Dodd drove on:

"Perrine claims you men are running wild, grabbing men you don't like and stringing them up in flat defiance of law and order. He says you've turned into an armed and vicious mob, and are threatening his life because he happens to be opposed to you politically—"

A rancher guffawed, without humor.

"He must figger he's got reason to fear us—this fine, former deputy U. S. marshal of yores," he rasped.

Dodd was not to be thrown off the track thus, however. He said:

269

"There's no doubt that you've banded together for unlawful purposes. You've come here, armed and ugly, to attack this jail. Perrine swears you're the moving spirit in this business, Hardesty. I'm sorry, but it's my duty to arrest you—"

The rest of his words was drowned out in an ominous roar of protest from Hardesty's companions. From the beginning they appeared to have regarded Lieutenant Dodd's intercession as no more than a check in what they intended doing. Not even yet would they give in to the idea that it was all over.

"Lay off uh that stuff, Dodd!" Lone Benton ejaculated. "Yuh ain't touchin' Hardesty. Not tonight!" And turning to Hardesty quickly: "We'll stand by yuh in this, Sale!"

It was an ugly moment. Lone was not single in his grim determination to prevent Hardesty's arrest if it came to that. The cowmen thrust forward, forbidding of mien. But Hardesty held up his hand.

"Hold it, boys," he advised. "You'll only get yourselves in trouble, resisting this officer. As he says, he's only doing his duty. It's a bitter dose, but I'll take my medicine; this ain't the end of the thing by a long shot."

Still Lone hesitated. As an army freighter in Texas, during his wild youth, he had lost all awe of the military; he had seen too many thick-witted officers put in their place by the hard-handed frontiersmen, without anything coming of it. But at Hardesty's warning gesture, he drew back, grumbling under his breath.

"Yo're bein' foolish about this, Sale!" he declared. "We know we're right. Dodd's makin' a big mistake. It ain't the first time he's crossed yuh without any better excuse," he added significantly.

If the remark conveyed anything to Hardesty, he gave no sign. Nor did he speak as two soldiers, at a word from the Lieutenant, stepped out smartly and started to take him in charge.

Before he could be relieved of his guns, however, an interruption occurred. A slim figure thrust out of the crowd which had gathered a little apart.

"Wait!" the clear voice rang out.

Lieutenant Dodd turned that way in surprise, as did Hardesty. Both recognized that voice. Nor were they mistaken. It was Glenna MacKinney who moved forward, quickly, but with calm assurance in her bearing. She met the officer's regard steadily.

"Mr. Dodd," she said levelly, "will you take my word for it that you are making a mistake?"

Dodd was disconcerted. "Is it you, Glenna?" he pretended surprise at the knowledge. His pause was awkward. And yet, his military training had not been for nothing. "It depends on what reasons you advance for the statement, I'm afraid."

The cowmen, alert for anything that would save the day, began to mutter at his stubbornness. "Nem'mine arguin' with the lady, Dodd!" one of them exclaimed. Hardesty attempted to spot Lone, lest he fire off some damaging broadside, but the Texan was not in evidence. Apparently he had withdrawn in disgruntlement.

Dodd was gazing at Glenna expectantly. Color began to show in the girl's face. Her lips were tight. Plainly she had never expected to come up against Dodd in his capacity as an army officer, and found him different from what she supposed. But she did not give up.

"Salem is quite right in what he says," she declared. "Rafe Perrine is a renegade. He deserves anything that might happen to him. I assure you, you are arresting the wrong man!"

Dodd evinced regret.

"I'm afraid there's nothing conclusive in what you say—" he began.

"Then I'll speak plainer. It was Perrine who instigated the murder of my father, Lieutenant!"

Dodd was frankly startled. "I heard something about that affair," he said slowly. "Perrine was present at the time, I know. But it was not he, but a drunken Indian, who—"

"Caused the actual shooting?" She was holding herself tense now, yet there was no faltering in her words. "That is right. But it was at Perrine's instruction."

The officer's skepticism was patent. Yet he strove to be fair, and succeeded only in being too pointedly patient.

"No, no, Glenna. I'm sorry—but it was the Indian's attack on Perrine which caused the whole business."

"Did it ever occur to you," Hardesty struck in as Dodd began to shake his head, "that that was exactly the way it was intended to appear?"

Dodd paused.

"It might be possible," he admitted. "But . . ."

Anger glinted in the girl's eyes now. "Must I tell you, Lieutenant, that Salem made it a point to find that Indian and get his story?" she demanded. At Dodd's inquiry, she related the occurrence, repeating Crow Feather's confession that he had acted throughout on Perrine's behalf, with the expectation of being rewarded with illicit whisky and a Spencer carbine.

Hearkening carefully, Dodd appeared impressed. He asked a number of questions. And then:

"Why wasn't this reported at the time, Glenna? Surely so serious a charge—your own father—"

Hardesty saved her from awkward explanations by interposing again.

"The first time I saw Perrine after I learned the truth, Dodd, I threw it up to him. He said what you know to be so: that nobody would believe an Indian. My hands were tied. Perrine had just been made a deputy marshal."

Dodd was further convinced. In the hope of clinching his conversation, Hardesty drove on:

"Another thing. There's the way Abe Slater died—the man who actually shot MacKinney. Who was it, killed him? Perrine! And why? Because he was the only man who knew the truth, whose word would carry weight . . . Perrine and Slater were cronies. Somehow Perrine persuaded Abe to give himself up—then shot him down without a chance for his life. All that evidence about Slater's making an attempt to escape jail could easily be manufactured. Perrine's story was the only evidence, and as he figured, nobody dreamed of questioning his word. I guessed the truth, but what good would it have done for me to speak up? . . . Perrine murdered Slater," he summed up flatly, "as coolly as he'd break a match—just to cover himself on the first murder!"

The cowmen listened to this in silent amazement. It was the first they had ever heard of Perrine's connection with the killing of Colin MacKinney. And while the trader meant little to most of them, the cold-bloodedness of it all whipped up their anger.

"By God, that's more'n enough!" Mart Pincher burst out furiously. "Perrine's a wolf, an' he don't deserve no better'n a wolf! Call yore soldiers aside, Dodd, an' we'll settle this!"

But Dodd, however convinced he might be that Perrine was all that he was painted, was far from

274

ready to comply. Under no circumstances did he propose to allow unbridled violence without lifting a hand to prevent it.

He stood there like a rock, barring the path to the jail.

"Whatever Perrine is," he made answer, "he is entitled to fair trial, the same as any man. I'm willing to do my best to see that he gets it." He paused, and it was plain that what he had to say now, came hard. But he did not shirk. "All this, bad as it is, has no connection with the present situation. Whether Perrine is a murderer or not, doesn't prove him a rustler—"

"Good God!" a rancher hurled at him violently. "Yuh know Perrine's a hydrophoby skunk! Do yuh need it in black an' white that he bites?"

Dodd demurred doggedly.

"Right now we're concerned with an attempted lynching," he declared. "Hardesty, I'm sorry to say, stands charged with incitement to riot . . ."

"Lieutenant!"

Glenna's single word cracked like a pistol-shot. Bright spots of color burned in her cheeks now. There could be no question that she was thoroughly aroused.

"Since when has it come to such a pass that a man must be arrested for demanding justice? Salem is entirely within his rights, as I know—and as you would understand, if you consider the facts with open mind. Rafe Perrine has made many attempts on him. By means of this systematic rustling he sought to ruin Salem, drive him from the country!"

Dodd followed her closely. He wasn't going to let sentiment sway him.

"It seems rather far-fetched—" he suggested.

"Not at all!" she denied stoutly. "Who but Salem Hardesty has opposed Perrine since he came to this country to practice his nefarious schemes? . . . *You* wouldn't know, Lieutenant; but it was Rafe Perrine who sold whisky and Spencer rifles to the Sioux, at the time when they were giving the army so much trouble! Salem Hardesty knew, though. It was he who broke up that business, and drove Perrine from the country—until he came back again, wearing the badge that protected him from stories which couldn't be proved . . . Ever since, Salem has opposed Perrine steadily, until Perrine was half mad with hatred.

"I see in your face that you do not believe. Well, even *I* refused to believe at first, Lieutenant. Salem faced Rafe Perrine at the trading post one Christmas Eve with an accusation of smuggling. Father and I drove him away. We were blind! But my eyes are open now, never to be closed again where Rafe Perrine is concerned. He is more dangerous than a rattlesnake—if I must say so, because such stubborn-willed men as you protect him!"

Hardesty listened to the flow of words astounded. Never had he expected Glenna to use such language to Dodd. Why, the two were as good as engaged—or so he had believed. His heart gave a bound at the thought that he might all along have been mistaken. The girl left little room for doubt concerning her attitude now, whatever it had been before. She was defending, not Lieutenant Dodd, but *him*—and doing it as though the outcome meant more to her than she would have been willing readily to admit.

As for Dodd, he stared at Glenna as if he could scarcely credit his ears.

"You mean what you say, Glenna," he managed huskily, his skin reddening, "and what you say is complete enough, God knows. If you think this much of Hardesty—" He found it impossible to go on.

Glenna perceived suddenly how far her fervor had carried her. A flush spread over her cheeks and throat, and anger and indignation dying out.

"I am thinking only of fairness," she said bravely, avoiding Hardesty's intent gaze. "If you arrest Salem under these circumstances, it will be the grossest injustice. Perhaps he and these other men have gone farther than they should. But surely they have had more than sufficient justification!"

Dodd withdrew warily from discussing the ethics of the situation with her.

"I'm willing to reconsider my decision to place you under arrest," he told Hardesty woodenly. "But you understand, this can't go on. I won't be responsible for what happens if it's carried any farther."

Hardesty knew a flash of admiration for the man in that moment. Dodd must realize completely what had happened here. It was far more than a matter of arresting or not arresting a man. He had just lost the girl he had been sure of for so long; unintentionally forcing Glenna to the test, he had watched her come fiercely to the defense of his rival. No man in his senses could have mistaken the significance of this.

And yet, Dodd was stanchly standing by his guns. As an army officer he could not countenance illegal acts of violence, whatever the justification.

"I haven't quite made up my mind about you as a whole," he pursued. "Perrine may have no right whatever to remain at large, but he has no reason to lie about the story which came to Fort Robinson tonight. What has almost happened here bears him out—"

"What yuh drivin' at?" Mart Pincher struck in gruffly. Dodd met his gaze squarely.

"I refer to these reported lynchings, Pincher. Did you stockmen catch a number of rustlers, and without recourse to the regular channels of organized law, hang them?"

Before the rancher could answer, Hardesty spoke up. "That's neither here nor there, Lieutenant," he insisted. "As you said earlier, it ain't the matter in hand!"

"Did you," Dodd repeated with flinty persistence, "apprehend and hang a number of men tonight?"

"Why, hell, no, Leftenant!" Pincher exclaimed gruffly. He had been quick to see Hardesty's reason for temporizing, and had no intention of allowing any damaging admissions from another quarter. "We ain't seen nobody tonight! Where'd yuh git that idee?"

Dodd stared at him suspiciously. Pincher's heartiness was a thought too bland, coming on top of what had passed.

"I dislike to question your word," he returned; "but I think you lie."

"Wal, that's yore privilege," Mart grinned, unabashed. "Matter o' fact, there was one gent we had a few words with. He was a rustler. He fired at one of my men without any warnin', an' was knocked over in self-defense. Before he cashed," he continued explanatorily, "he told us a few things about Perrine that settled all our doubts about Rafe . . . Reason we come here, so help me, was to ask him a few questions."

Dodd was not amused. "That may be," he retorted curtly. "I must refuse to allow you to carry out your plan. In fact," an edge stole into his voice, "I'm afraid I must instruct you to disperse."

For a moment, silence fell. It had come at last—the flat failure of their intentions. The cowmen looked at one another, faces darkening.

"Like hell we will!" one began ominously. "We come here to dicker with that buzzard, an'—"

Hardesty had long since given in to the inevitable. However accounts were to be squared with Perrine, it was not here and this way. While it irked him that Glenna must wait still longer before she saw her father's account stand squared on the books, he had no intention of allowing any unbridled violence, least of all while she was present. He started to reason with the cowmen, but they were not inclined to listen. Their grievance against Perrine, plus what they had learned about him in the last half hour, had brought them to a pitch where nothing less than vengeance would satisfy them.

They were muttering still, an ominous note in their voices, when a stir occurred at the rear. Hardesty turned to learn what was the cause of it, and spotted Lone. The Texan was beckoning to him earnestly. Hardesty made toward him.

"Come on, Sale—do as Dodd says," he urged in a harsh whisper as Hardesty came close. His next words electrified everyone within hearing. "I've got Perrine!"

"What!"

Hardesty made sure Lieutenant Dodd understood nothing of what was afoot, and then led Lone farther away, followed by the others. Lone repeated:

"I got Perrine! While yuh was chewin' the rag, I busted in the back of the jail. Perrine was there, hidin' like the coyote he is. We come together an' I slugged 'im . . . I got 'im tied on a bronc now, in the brush a hundred yards back of the jail!"

Something burst over these men like a flame at the news. They tightened up in a flash. "Swell!" Mart Pincher breathed. "By grab, we'll settle that gent's hash in short order! Let's get goin'!"

CHAPTER TWENTY

"Hold it!" Hardesty warned before the rush could start.

"Don't be in a sweat about this. Break up slow, as if you didn't like it a bit—"

They saw his point. Almost casually, with much pretended disgruntlement, the cowmen began to separate and move off. Hardesty turned back to Glenna.

"I'll see you home, Glenna," he told her.

She smiled her consent. Whatever Lieutenant Dodd's thoughts were as he watched the pair move off, he kept them to himself. Bitter as it had been for him, he had done his duty as he saw it and must abide by the consequences.

It was not far to the store, yet Hardesty could not forget the thought of Rafe Perrine, waiting, bound to his horse, in the brush behind the jail. He didn't want to see Perrine hanged. It would be a mistake to admit the fact before these cowmen who had suffered so long at the other's hands. But he thought perhaps if he could reach Perrine in time, he could avert violence—see that Perrine paid the price prescribed by law for such crimes as his. The need to act quickly and keep his wits about him made him silent, tense.

Glenna caught that, if the cause of it was hidden from her. She had no inkling of what was afoot. At the store she made it plain that she expected Hardesty to step in. When he made no move to do so, she scanned his features anxiously.

"What is it, Salem?" she asked. "What is troubling you?"

He couldn't tell her. He said rapidly: "I'll leave you now. I've something I must do."

She stepped back. "Of course, if you must—"

He took a deep breath. "I'll return as soon as I can," he promised. His swift glance swept the street as he swung into the saddle. Few cowmen were in evidence. He knew what they were doing; it spurred him to haste.

Turning down the side of the store toward the brush, Hardesty almost ran into a group of waiting horsemen. Lone Benton was with them, and Mart Pincher.

"That you, Sale?" Lone whispered. "Let's go, then—" He was strung taut. No more was said as he led the way through the brush.

Quickly they worked their way toward the rear of the jail. Other cowmen joined them quietly; the group which had broken up so quietly before the jail, was soon re-assembled.

"Where is Perrine?" Hardesty asked Lone. The Texan pointed toward the shadowy line of brush along a creek bottom.

"Down there. I tied up his bronc where it

wouldn't be found in a hurry if anythin' happened—"

They pressed forward quickly. Lone jogged along the line of alders, peering. He seemed at a loss for the moment. Finally he pointed again.

"In that patch there, I reckon . . ."

It proved empty, however. The cowmen turned on Lone impatiently. "What the hell here, Benton! Yuh ain't tryin' to put somethin' over on us! Yuh did git Perrine, like yuh say?"

"Shore I got 'im!" Lone insisted. "Hold on, now. Mebby that ain't the spot—" His shrewd glance probed the brush clumps, remarkably alike in the blanketing gloom. "Look down there," he muttered, pointing with his chin.

Hardesty had already begun to feel some uneasiness. His tight-strung nerves warned him that something was wrong. It was not like Lone to be vague in such a matter; certainly he wouldn't do it purposely.

Rusty Gallup and one of the Circle P men returned from the clump Lone had indicated. They had found nothing. Distrustful looks were bent on Lone now.

"What the hell kind of a stunt is this?" a man rasped. "Perrine's got away on yuh, Benton!"

Lone had been struggling with himself silently. At this he gave over.

"That's the answer," he grunted. "I put him in the bushes there, where I showed yuh first. I'm shore of it. Somehow he got out of his ropes!"

"Then right now he's makin' fer Wyomin' or the Dakota country tight as that bronc can take 'im!" It was thrown out fiercely, a blunt accusation. "Dang yuh, Benton—!"

Lone whirled on the speaker. "Lay off, Cade!" he warned thinly. "If it wa'n't fer me, Perrine'd still be safe in the jail! I done the best I could, an' a dang sight more'n you . . ."

Hardesty broke up the bickering in short order. "It don't matter how it happened," he pointed out curtly, "Perrine's got away from us. Every minute we chew the rag puts him that much farther away from us! What we've got to do now is track him down and finish our job!"

"Yo're right, Hardesty."

"Cut the chatter an' let's get goin'!" the voices seconded.

As the best tracker in the bunch, Hardesty pushed toward the first brush clump Lone had indicated. Warning the others to keep back, he dismounted and pushed in. His examination was brief. The sulphur match flickered out and he rose.

"He was left here all right," he announced. "Somehow he broke loose and untied his bronc. He headed across the creek."

They started that way. Making a torch of dry brush, Hardesty searched the farther bank. A set of pony tracks struck away toward the north.

"Makin' fer the Black Hills," Mart Pincher commented. Hardesty's nod was one of agreement. He scanned the sky.

"There's a couple hours of dark left. We'll shove north and try to pick up Perrine's trail as soon as we can see."

Without ado, they headed north and shoved the horses to a brisk pace. Hardesty clung to the easy going, even when it threw him to one side a mile or so, believing that to be the course a fugitive would take. Except for an occasional muttered word, the men rode in grim silence.

They were still pressing forward when the first faint light cracked the eastern horizon and slowly widened. A rosy glow crept up the sky. Half an hour later the shadows melted like mist and it was possible to see.

At Hardesty's suggestion, the cowmen spread out. There was no trace of Perrine's passing to be found. Lines of worry began to appear in the flat faces of the men. But Hardesty was nothing if not methodical.

"Work off to the west," he proposed colorlessly, at Mart Pincher's hasty ejaculation to the effect that Perrine had given them the slip. "Until we know he's had time to reach the Canadian border, there's still a chance to nab him."

They did as he directed. For a time it appeared that even this must fail. Then the flat, muted double-crack of a signal shot sounded. It came from a mile or two west. Hardesty tightened up once more. He knew there was a chance that Perrine might hear the signal and be warned; but now was no time to waste the minutes.

Ten minutes later he joined a group waiting on the slope of a low ridge. Lone Benton grinned wolfishly at him. He pointed to the ground.

"There yuh are, Sale! I knowed we'd never lose him. His luck ain't that good—"

Sure enough, there lay the tracks of a hard-driven pony, making into the northwest. Miles beyond, the dark bulge of the first hills caught the warm splash of the morning sun.

Hardesty took time to examine the tracks with care. "Made a couple of hours ago, perhaps less," he remarked, straightening. The fact reassured him. It meant that Perrine was driving his mount beyond reason. The animal would wear down just that much sooner. Then it could be overhauled easily.

By midmorning the pines clothing the hills, match-high in the distance, could be made out. Perrine was making for the wooded ridges as if cover about him would lessen his fear of pursuit. There was something strange in the thought which gave Hardesty pause. He had never known Perrine to lose his head, and was unwilling to believe that was the case now.

Another thought came: Perrine, in his gun-running days, had come to know these hills intimately. The fact had not occurred to Hardesty before. Yet if ever Perrine was to depend on his knowledge of the country to save his life, it was now. What did the hills offer in the way of defense, of which they were ignorant?

They learned before long, when Perrine's trail ran out on a flinty area where little but the scratches of hoofs on stone could be seen. It was a long, uneven slope, and Perrine could have turned in several directions to throw them off. Did he know how close they were behind him? Even now, Hardesty reflected, he might be watching narrowly from some high point of vantage, rifle in hand, waiting for the first man to push unsuspectingly within range.

Dropping to the ground, Hardesty made a thorough search. Only those faint scratches where iron shoes had scraped the rocks gave him the clue. For several minutes he was puzzled at the point where Perrine had drawn in briefly, whirling his horse perhaps to gaze backward. Presently he found where the other had struck away, angling up the slope in a westerly direction.

"He made for that gap yonder," Hardesty grunted, swinging into the hull.

If the climb was not easy, neither had it been so for their quarry. Hardesty wasted no time in verifying his findings: Perrine would not have wasted any in altering his intentions.

This rugged slope was the base of a wooded

height above; the gap which Hardesty had indicated, led ever upward between bold bastions of rock. There was plenty of cover up there, and Hardesty grew wary at the increasing danger of ambush. Others were thinking the same thoughts. Yet none hung back for that reason.

Reaching the rocky portals of the gap, they drew rein to stare. Above rose a veritable granite ladder, up and up, merging fifty yards beyond with the pines. If it was a trail it was one of the worst in existence.

"Perrine never come this way!" Mart Pincher exclaimed. "A hoss couldn't make it, Hardesty—"

However, after a brief scrutiny the latter nodded doggedly. "He came this way all right," he insisted. "Here's his sign, pointin' straight up!"

Lone Benton hesitated, staring, and his jaw dropped. "Wal, dang me, was I fool 'nough to give him a bronc that could make that?" he burst out.

"It's a trap!" Red Tyler threw in warningly. "There must be some way around, Hard! . . . If we tackle that, Perrine's shore to be layin' up there, ready to knock us off one at a time!"

"You may be right," Hardesty nodded grimly. "All I want to know is that he's up there."

He was the first to start up. Half a dozen yards on the slick rock and he slid to the ground, leading his pony. Despite their muttering, the others followed without hesitation. Soon they were strung out along the trail, busily scrambling from one unstable surface to the next. The trail was none too wide. In places it was nearly non-existent.

Momently Hardesty expected the rocks to echo to the crash of a rifle. All knew that Perrine carried one. Lone had relieved him of his six-gun, but had left the rifle in its saddle-scabbard on his pony. That mistake might well cost them dearly before Perrine was finally taken—if he ever was.

Under the ardent blaze of the noon-day sun, they crept steadily higher. Ladder was a good name for this trail; it was like scrambling from rung to rung, with nothing but space between. At long last Hardesty began to approach the top. Unwarningly, then, a shot rang out.

Hardesty heard the vicious flutter past his shoulder; lead smeared the rock, and whined away. In a flash he flung up his gun and fired toward the trees. It was answered quickly. Behind him, Lone yelled warning. Hardesty did not even hear it, except as a meaningless sound. Dropping the reins of his bronc, he sprang forward.

The quickness of his move saved the cowmen from being knocked off like bottles on a fence. Alarmed, Perrine fired repeatedly at his flitting form—missing again and again. Hardesty was near the top now. With a last plunge, he reached the cover of a gnarled pine grappling the rocks for support, and drew himself up. Perrine he knew was hidden within a dozen yards. Yet he held his fire.

It was the uncertainty which got Perrine. When Hardesty reached his hiding-place five minutes later, the quarry had fled. Hardesty whirled. The cowmen had come on doggedly; Lone bringing his horse up. It was not possible to ride here, but Hardesty led the way up the needle-strewn slope to better going. A moment later he got a flash of Perrine, fleeing across the hollows. That his mount was far spent was patent from the manner in which he drove it.

Swiftly the pursuit closed in. Still Perrine showed a wolfish wariness, dodging through the pines in bewildering fashion. Repeatedly he disappeared completely. It was anybody's guess what his next move would be.

"Spread out!" Hardesty called. "Don't let him circle back!"

Two minutes later a sudden crash of shots to the right flung him that way. Lone Benton had cornered Perrine. Hardesty caught a glimpse of his grim face as he closed in. Then he saw Perrine. Turning like a wounded grizzly, Rafe sprang toward Lone as if he meant to ride him down. The rifle in his hands spat wickedly.

An expression of amazement spread over Lone's leathery features. He jerked in the saddle, caught himself. But he had been hit. Hardesty cried out, to distract Perrine's attention:

"Drop your gun, Perrine!"

Rafe whirled. There was a madness of hate and rage in his face. He saw Hardesty. Every ounce of venom in him concentrated on his enemy. Without bringing his rifle to his shoulder, he fired. The slug tore through Hardesty's shirt, clipping his ribs.

Hardesty delayed long enough to make sure of his aim. He fired once. Perrine jerked as though stung. Even as he stiffened, the rifle slid out of his hands. He never stopped his horse, tumbling forward out of the hull as it ran. His body struck the ground like a log, rolled over till it brought up against a gnarled pine, and then slumped back. He did not move again.

Hardesty built a new house on the 6 Lightning that fall. It went up quickly, and was finished before snow flew. That he was proud of it could have been told from his talk.

Glenna knew about it. Though she had not seen it as yet, she followed the progress of its building with interest on the occasions when Hardesty rode to town. And these were frequent now. With the rustling broken up, and the round-up put behind, there fell a quiet spell. Hardesty made the most of it.

On one of the last, warm, sunny days of

October, he put in an appearance in MacKinney with an extra bronc. Glenna was expecting him. The new ranch house had been completed the week before, and the girl had accepted an invitation to ride out and see it.

Leaving the store in charge of a man Glenna could trust, they started without loss of time. It was a beautiful day, the sky a soft deceptive blue, the brown buffalo grass of the range nodding in the breeze.

Both were in the best of spirits. Glenna seemed to have put sadness behind her of late; her eyes were bright with interest, her manner almost expectant. Hardesty felt much the same. He had waited long to ask this girl a question whose answer meant everything to him. Even today he hesitated.

He knew Glenna had not seen Lieutenant Dodd since the occurrences at the jail. That in itself was promising. But Hardesty was not disposed to take anything for granted. One false step, he told himself, and he might lose Glenna forever.

She had always liked the lay of the land about the 6 Lightning. It was indeed picturesque, with its open parks, its rocky knolls, and clumps of pine. She had told him before, and now repeated, that she thought he possessed the finest ranch the country could offer. Hardesty nodded assent.

"I could make out to spend the rest of my life here without any regrets," he observed.

They came within sight of the house presently. Glenna's eyes lit up. "Salem!" she exclaimed. "Why, that must be the finest place this side of Sidney."

"Well, I didn't spare any expense," he admitted.

It was the same inside. Glenna moved from room to room, her admiration unchecked. Almost every window gave upon a pleasant prospect of pine-clad hills. Far beyond, to the south, rose the white cliffs of the Niobrara. "What a beautiful home," she said. There could be little doubt that she meant it.

"I like it now." He pretended casualness in the words. "Of course the day may come when I—"

She turned toward him.

"Yes, Salem?"

He avoided her glance. "Well, I was a trapper for years, Glenna. It's a breed that's known for its wandering."

"You mean you might someday get the desire to move on?" There was a trace of anxiety in her tone.

"That's about it—"

Still he neglected to meet her gaze. Not even he could escape the knowledge that the moment for which he had waited so long was here at last. How could he make use of it? Never a man of many words, he distrusted himself.

She was silent so long that at last he turned

despite himself. To his amazement, there was a smile on her lips.

"I know what you are thinking, Salem," she told him steadily. "You are afraid you will have to live here alone—that the day may come when you can stand it no longer. Then you'll be forced to leave. Am I right?"

He nodded, wordless. Not even the haze before his own eyes prevented him from seeing the tenderness in hers. Her understanding laugh bubbled, and that was too much for him.

When she spoke again, it was from the depths of his arms, which had swiftly encircled her and drawn her close.

"Did you think I would let you get away from me now?" she chided softly, nestling against him. "This is your home, Salem, but it is mine too! I knew from the moment you started building it that I should have to live here. Now I am more sure of it than ever, my dear!"

She could not have added more had she wanted to, for her lips were prisoners at last.

| Books are produced in the United States using U.S.-based materials | Books are printed using a revolutionary new process called THINKtech™ that lowers energy usage by 70% and increases overall quality | Books are durable and flexible because of Smyth-sewing | Paper is sourced using environmentally responsible foresting methods and the paper is acid-free |

Center Point Large Print
600 Brooks Road / PO Box 1
Thorndike, ME 04986-0001 USA

(207) 568-3717

US & Canada:
1 800 929-9108
www.centerpointlargeprint.com